PO

G000126418

POLLUTED SEX

Polluted Sex

Lauren Foley

Lauren Foley

Influx Press
London

Published by Influx Press
The Greenhouse
49 Green Lanes, London, N16 9BU
www.influxpress.com / @InfluxPress
All rights reserved.
© Lauren Foley, 2022

First edition 2022. Printed and bound in the UK by TJ Books.

Paperback ISBN: 9781910312919
Ebook ISBN: 97819103125766

Editors: Sanya Semakula, Dan Coxon
Proofreader: Trudi Suzanne Shaw
Cover design: Sukruti Anah Staneley
Interior design: Vince Haig

Contents

Penitential Acts	7
Mammy Mary Says	9
Blue	17
Purple With Mottled Black	27
Hot Rocks	37
Hills Like Hemingway's	45
Pinna	53
Before Him	55
These Young Things	75
The Perfect Flick	83
Polluted Sex	95
Formalism…	125
The First Person Possessive	127
Phonology	137
Interlude Belles-Lettres	139
Diktat/Dictate I	151
Joni Mitchell Nudes	153
Molly & Jack At The Seaside	155
Winona the Wicked Wanton Woman	165
ABCB AABCCB// Untitled Child's Song	179
How, I?	185
Squiggly Arse Crack	189
Axis	195
Let Ashore	197
Pivot	205
Diktat/Dictate II	207
Churching	209

'For my Nanny, Essie, my Granny, Kitty, and my Mam, Patricia; some women for three women xxx'

Penitential Acts

Breathless. Spoken.
/ = beat
// = pause
— = run-on lines
: // = abrupt pause

I confess to almighty God / and to you / my brothers and
sisters / that I have sinned through my own fault / in my
thoughts and in my words / in what I have done / and in
what I have failed to do / and I ask blessèd Mary / ever
Virgin / all the angels and saints / and you / my brothers
and sisters / to pray for me to the Lord our God / in the
upper echelons of this faith they drink the fruits / our
earthly labour / which human hands hath made / begotten
not made / of one being with the Father / / Lie here / /
striking shadows cast by clouds turning and twisting above
/ me / Stretch out / on backs considering skyscape /
plucked from the vine / grapes / which human hands have
made / see through its taut transparent skin / see its veins /
peel back the burgundy cover / succulent and wet to its core
/ in my / where the seed is hard / in my thoughts / covered
by this fleshy extremity / in my thoughts / the oval spot
concealed by this flesh / blessèd flesh / in my thoughts /
blessèd are you among women / in what I have done / in
thought / and blessèd is the fruit of your womb / / sunkissed
/ / And in what I have failed to do—weather-beaten fruitless

harvest a decrepitude of old men's impotence—what have I
what have I done—lonely only beauty of youth—I ask—full
of plucking ripe for the picking—pluck my impotence of
now—what have I done—I have done—subdue the music
be with the heart the bosom—lie down—here—under our
earthly labour—I have done undone—I have warmed to the
flicker with heat and move next to me in the vine we are one
to be done and undone—what have I—I have // burned
with the dance and you're close so close so close the ripeness
lie here on your back rest lay your head on me you are ripe
for the plucking from this vine and music be the heart of
dance and: // what have I have have done I have done and:
// the fruit of this vine is next to be plucked by hands we
have made and ready to pluck the flesh your flesh my flesh
and lubricate ourselves and the fruit of the union spontaneous
growth—fruition—we consecrate this vine with a stupor a
passion a flame a hell and Burn Burn Burn for all your mortal
sins ashes to ashes dust to dust—a new test— // And I ask
blessèd Mary all the angels and saints to pray for us sinners
now and at the hour of our death: // through our fault
through our fault through our most grievous fault

Mammy Mary Says

Your Best Friend and you are on your way to her house. It's a bit cold and you're both wearing earmuffs. She lives in the Council Estate closest to your Primary School. You do think it's pretty special to have a Best Friend. It is a soft thing. Like her. Her black curly hair and her giggly laugh. She's very smiley which is a nice way for a Best Friend to be. You know not all the girls have Best Friends – maybe just the twins and Cara and Elaine, and youse two. Youse've been thick as thieves since day one of Junior Infants, cos you were both too shy to put up your hands and ask: *An bhfuil cead agam dul go dtí an leithreas, más é do thoil é?* Mrs Swan was dead nice and didn't make a fuss, she just gave yis spare knickers from her clothes chest up the front at Little Breaktime. It could have been dead scarlet for yis, but Swanny was always great about making nothing out of something. That first day of Primary School was also your fourth birthday, and you're only a day and a month older than your Best Friend which is pretty special too.

When youse are alone yis do play loads of deadly makey-uppy games, dress up in your Mam's old clothes and have the gas talking really posh like about 'just a sli-ver of cake', and youse do learn dance rou-tines to your favourite songs youse'd never ever show to anyone else. Youse do often play hopscotch or skipping too—because they are her favourites. And when youse do have to line-up outside, on the tarmac yard, every morning, before roll call, you're always saying about the stories in Soaps off of the TV, you do draw rubbish pictures of the charact-ers at home with silly word bubbles in an old copy book, and show them only to her, and when youse were old enough to get pocket money she even agreed to spend some of hers on comics—because that's what you wanted to do. See, she is best for lots and lots of reasons.

So youse watched this cartoon kind of a video in Primary School after lunch today. Miss Kane showed it only for the girls in Fourth Class; and there were cartoon girls who grew into grown-up girls. Your Best Friend is laughing now, as youse're mos-ey-ing to her house, about the boobs on the TV, sticking her chest out and tripping over her feet with the giggles. Then youse're skipping up The Avenue of semi-private houses and ducking at front walls and hedges and scooting past gates with your chests pushed way out and falling over laughing. You take off your white earmuffs and say: *This is my bra,* and twist and place it so the two muffs make two boobs. And she looks at you—eyes out on stalks—her cheeks pink; then takes her purple ones off and does the same. Youse're laughing like mad things now. Proper giggle fit.

As you pass by Marianne Stewart's house, whose Dad works for the Union, your Best Friend straightens her back and starts walking dead funny—like that mous-tach-i-o-ed man Basil Fawlty off of the telly—because Marianne's Mam is very strict and never lets her even outside their front gate to play. Never. Not even after school on a Friday; AND her Mam doesn't let ANY child inside their house either. Ever. If you want to play with Marianne after school you can only play in her front garden, with the gate shut, when it's not raining; and Marianne's a bit snooty too, living on The Avenue, and you aren't too bothered with her, but your Best Friend has to sit with her in class and likes her, so you'd often have to play with her for your Best Friend.

You live five or six fields away from The Avenue. Your Dad is a Farmer. Or, well, he was. He works for the Civil Service down the Country now. You think it must be a lot less fun of a job. He is working down there since he did a Bad Sin, and your Mam won't let him sleep in your house. He comes up once during the week to take your Grandad to the Market, and you and your Little Brother do see him the evening before, in the sitting room, for one hour. Your Big Brother and Sister don't have to see him; and your Mam doesn't ever talk to him. Sometimes you do sneak out of the sitting room to find your Mam in the kitchen, to show her that you're on her side; but she just sends you back in then with the teapot and mugs, and a cup and saucer for your Dad, on the wheelie trolley.

When your Dad comes to the Village for Market, and at weekends, he stays in his old room in your Grandad's house from when he was little himself, you had never ever seen the upstairs bedrooms until he moved back in there and you can't believe your Grandparents, Aunties and Uncles slept in two rooms that small.

You know what the Bad Sin is your Dad did. Your Little Brother doesn't know. So, you're not allowed to talk about it, not even to your Best Friend. It does be weird in school when the Teachers are going on about the Commandments because you know your Dad did one of those BIG SINS, and you do feel like you shouldn't like your Dad because he's a Sinner who Sinned against your Mam; but you do also like your Dad, because, well, he's your Dad. And, you love him. You love your Dad.

Your Mam has told you they are sep-ar-a-ted. You know marriage is for life, and no one else's parents are separated, in fact, you'd never even heard of it before, you know it is against the Church, and you think it is against the Law; so, you do just go on thinking he's still your Dad who lives near to his new job. And, because you're not allowed to talk about it, it's easy to pretend none of it is true at all.

The only thing that makes it hard to pretend is you know your Mam doesn't have much money on her own. And, even though youse still live in your private house on your Grandad's fields, you know that your Mam gets Social Welfare for youse all now; you think this must be something bad like a Sin because you're not allowed to talk about it either. Your Mam is a-shame-d, and doesn't want people knowing. Things aren't really that different except you go to a different Dentist and you don't go to the Doctor in The Village anymore, but to the Health Clinic in the bigger Town nearby. What you really don't like is when your Mam makes you and your Little Brother cycle all the way to that Town, there's loads of hard hills that ache your legs, because she says yis can't afford the bus now.

Your Dad takes you and your Little Brother to the Airport on Sunday afternoons, youse do have to go through se-cur-i-ty even though you're not getting on a plane. Your Dad knows the Guard, so he makes a big show of checking you and your Little Brother for IRA bombs with his handheld scanner thingy, then youse run down to the wide long cor-ri-dor with all the windows and watch the planes flying in and out. Youse do go get food and your Dad always gets youse minerals and makes youse promise not to tell your Mam. You do look at your Little Brother, like youse should just have tea like yis are let; but then he looks at you like go on we'll have the minerals—and he has a cheeky smile and you want him to be happy—so you do just nod. What you're really thinking is: there goes your Dad with another Sin, again.

When you do see your Dad these days, he is too ser-i-ous, he does always be wearing suits; but your Grandad only wears suits to Mass on Sundays, and Mass is never ever fun so your Dad's job must be awful awful. Your Grandad is still a Farmer and you love love love out the back of his house. There are broken old Ford tractors and you and your Little Brother are let climb and skit on them as if yis could drive or harvest the potatoes, which does be gas. Your Grandad wears working slacks with round-collared shirts, knitted cardigans and keeps material hankies in his pockets not paper tissues. He also wears a flat cap in the glasshouses, and keeps his dark grey taller hat for with his Sunday suit. You think he has the best man's job; and when you give him your kisses hello and goodbye he always smells of outside.

Your Best Friend and you are nearly at the corner to turn right onto her road and you notice she's stopped laughing and has taken her pretend purple bra off, you keep saun-ter-ing past doing a silly walk like an Egyptian while keeping hold of your white bra under your chin and wiggling your bum and shaking your chest. She yanks your arm and says: *No. Stop!* You whip your head around to look at her face. She looks like she'll cry. And she never ever ever cries. You remember even the time her Dad—who works for the County Council—took the bamboo stick down off the top of the TV Unit and hit her with it on the underside of her two stockinged feet, and she just looked at him like nothing had happened. Hah. You were dead proud of her then. You know that Dads have to hit kids when they are bold, and your Dad even used to use his belt, until your Mam stopped him doing that; and you also know, because Miss Kane said so, that Teachers hitting kids is against the Law now. Other than his bamboo stick your Best Friend's Dad is lots of fun. He gets up very early to work for the County Council, actually he is a Bin

Man. Your Best Friend thinks this is a little em-barr-ass-ing and sometimes sings a song about her old man the dustman; but you don't think it is embarrassing. It's a job like any other job and it means he gets home from work in the daytime.

When he comes home he spends time with youse. He always asks about what youse've been playing and smiles and makes jokes, and sometimes he sits down and plays with yis on the landing. Your Dad never plays kids' games.

A little bit, you are scared of her Dad, because he keeps ferrets in hutches out the back, and he knows you think they are UGLY and MAD. You're not really scared of him, but of the rotten ferrets, and he finds it really funny to bring youse outside when he's feeding them and let them run up his leg. He does say they are terrible bad biters and he must be careful that they don't scoot up inside his trousers and bite his ghoulies, and laughs a lot. Then he does pretend, every time, to throw one to you, and you do jump backwards, and everyone laughs. You really wish they would just have a dog or a cat like the rest of the Village.

Your Mam went to their house re-cent-ly to collect you, which was a bit weird, because usually your Big Brother collects you when he's coming in from *'causing havoc'* with his friends. She was inside in the kitchen with your Best Friend's Mam and Dad for ages, youse didn't mind because yis got to play until later, but you knew when everyone was saying goodbye that your Mam must have been talking to them about the Big Sin because of how they all looked at you in a slow sad way.

Your Best Friend will be moving to the Village soon, into a semi-private house, you were really put out about this at first because you thought that she would have to change schools but then other kids from the Council Estate beside your school were also moving and a minibus was a-rrange-d by your school for when those houses will get built. So you'll still get to play in each other's houses on Friday afternoons, which is great.

By the way, that time your Best Friend's Dad hit her with his bamboo stick youse were only whispering, but her Mam, Mary, who doesn't have a job job—other than being a Mam, kept moaning because she couldn't hear Coronation Street. Yeah so, what you mean is, most all of the girls' Mams are housewives usually with some-of-the-time jobs. Nearly all of the Dads have a job; or they do try to have one. Since last school year there's a girl who moved all the way out here from Town-Town and her parents are REALLY young—and she's an ONLY CHILD. Imagine! Imagine how quiet her house must be. So, this girl's Mam has bobbed hair; and a job of her own in Town-Town. She goes in and out to TOWN every day. You think it's in like a Bank or something. In anyways it's not a job in the Village, or a some-of-the-time job from her own house, or another woman's house. It's not a job like cleaning, ironing, sewing, or minding kids—it's a job like a Dad's job. You think she could be an A-ccoun-tant. Or maybe nearly an Accountant, cos maybe you heard she has to do more tests. Who cares! She has a Dad's job! She has her own shiny black briefcase, much much nicer than your Dad's gicky wine one, wears make-up on weekdays, and you do think she blow-dries her hair every morning, because it always looks soft, and oh! it's blonde, you forgot to say it's all blondie and fancy. You don't even remember what this girl's Dad does; because it was so so cool to hear that her Mam had a Dad's job, you stopped even listening to all what the other girls were asking about.

Your Best Friend wants to be a Wife and a Mam when she grows up. You don't; you do think it is a hard life, with no money. You don't know yet what job you want to have; but you do know you do not want to be a Teacher. You like your Teachers a lot, and they like you because you are quiet and always do your ecker. Mrs Swan has her own kids and Miss Kane doesn't. You can only have kids if you're Married. You know you def-i-nite-ly don't want to end up sad and poor like your Mam if your Husband does a Big Sin, and you're really not all that mad into minding kids or playing with dolls. Being a Teacher looks a lot like being a Mam to heaps and heaps of kids. No thank you very much! You really like drawing and playing and dancing, but messing is not a job so you still do not know what you would like to be. But, you love your Best Friend. You love your Best Friend's sweet soft smiley face and don't want her to cry; so you do a funny dance and start going around the corner again. She hits you on the arm. Her cheeks are bright red, she says: *My. Mam. My. Mam. Might. See. Us.* Your Best Friend really might cry. You feel squishy and sick but your head feels full and tight at the exact same time. You look at her and say: *It's ok. It's funny.* She chews her lip and says: *No ...*

You take your white bra off and put your mittened *lámh* out, then your Best Friend puts her mittened *lámh* in yours. Youse walk on around the corner—hand-in-hand—together, turn the key in the poxy brown front door, go into her house and on down to the kitchen and Mammy Mary is at the half-opened back door pretending she wasn't smoking her John Player Blue. She tells youse she's going to make tea and toast – with grilled cheese on it; which is more than a bit special. Youse smile at each other.

And Mammy Mary says: '*Girls, wash your dirty hands.*'

Blue

I haven't slept properly in nearly four months. It was Summer when this started. It's almost Christmas now. I am woozy and washy every night when I lie down. My head spins, full of music, the day's events, conversations, daydreams, teachers droning, and needle-like pains. I listen to the phone-in show on FM104. There is usually only one voice at a time, when no one is arguing, and I can trick my head into focusing on those singular words as they're uttered, not on the meanings, just the one voice talking, and the calm down, calm tones of the host. I listen in the dark until my sister, who's grown and working, comes in to sleep. I lie here all the early night hours listening. Quieting.

Sarah is off school sick today and I think maybe I have her virus, I ask the teacher can I go to the loo, some of the girls ask every class, that's the cool thing to do, they go alternately, leave notes for each other on top of high-level cisterns, smoke out the windows. I hate going to the toilet in school, they're right down the end of the Old Corridor. It is always fucking arctic. The walk down the hall equals instantaneous goosebumps under gabardine skirt, above scratchy knee socks right up to my flowery *Penneys* cotton knickers, I pull them down, cursing the cold, there's a dry dark brown streak staining the gusset.

When I'm lying in bed awake after midnight I have these momentary drops, falls, waves that shock me out of the sleep my body longs to fall into. They are horrifically scary, I fear them so much—that at times—I push further into the exhaustion.

At little breaktime I walk around the smaller schoolyard with Tina. We walk round and round on a loop for twelve of the fifteen minutes resembling two young women our age in the parlour of a 19th Century novel. She keeps asking me if I'm ok, but I don't want to talk about it, I bark, turn, turn, turn as we reach each grass verge. When the bell sounds I come over all fainty and realise Tina is holding me up. She deftly passes me a note later, when we are moving between classes, saying I look like a ghost me, that I'm sick and need to go home to bed. But, I can't go home because there's no one at home so the school won't let me, my Mam is at work cleaning a rich woman's house and won't be free until home time. She stays late to do extra ironing on Wednesdays. I know she needs the money, that's her own separate money. I can last a few more hours.

o

I never tell my mother or my sister about the misplaced shit stain. Two months later there is brightening on my knickers. Blotted, not streaked. I take them off, and change into one of the black pairs my Mam gave me for this purpose, I fold a clean flannel from the hot press inside, hold the sullied knickers in my hands, call my sister into the bedroom and show her. She starts to cry. I think to myself she shouldn't be the one crying; but I really, honestly, feel numb. My mother comes in and all is hugs and kisses. Such a fuss is made. I'm given an adhesive sanitary towel. My sister says I'm so lucky I don't have to wear the old-style pads she had to on her first friend. Friend! The ones with a belt and loops that felt like a facecloth between your legs. I think she knows I stole the flannel, that it's underneath me now, I make a plan to bury it or dump it out in the back field, I start thinking I'll have to take it somewhere even further away; but where, where could I ever hide this bloodied rag? I remember the long detachable two-inch-thick pads she's mentioned from *Are You There God? It's Me, Margaret*, the belt sounded like a right contraption. The girls in school use *Always*. I hope I won't be given some generic cheaper brand. Sometimes there are own-brand yellow and black boxes in my parents' room, which would be mortifying to take to school. My Mam tells me she will get me *Tampax*, for next time, because they are more comfortable to wear for girls my age, but pads will do for now. She mentions about putting the tampons inside me, which I already knew about from diagrams in magazines, but hearing her talk about applicators and non-applicators makes me want to vomit. There is warm red blood coming out of me and I will have to put something inside that private part of me every month. I will have to touch the inside of it. I really, honestly, feel numb. And weak and tired, so very very tired. And light, so light, which kind of feels like happy. It's awfully confusing.

o

Last Summer, around the same time as the beginnings of sleeplessness, these other feelings started not unlike the washy feelings, not unlike the prickly feelings, but their very own kind of feelings, like a change in temperature when someone enters a room, but inside and outside of my body, these new … sensations … I do not have the vocabulary to describe.

I would take to reading on my parents' double bed in the afternoons, it was always quiet there, the light was better than in my bottom bunk, and if I was lucky no one realised where I was for a few hours. The cover of Molly Keane's *Good Behaviour* peeked out at me from one stack of books lining the skirting. It's a painting of a woman dancing, and I like how she looks, different, not from right now; not quite from *The House of Eliott* my sister and I watch on TV either. I like her face, she isn't necessarily pretty, but I would like to look like her. I like the roundedness of her lower body, her shapeliness. My body heat fluctuates when I see her – a different kind of heat altogether. She always catches my eye. I might say I find her attractive. I don't know why because she's far from stunning; but she is nice to look at. I worry though that I look at her too long or too often. I don't think it's out of vanity. I like how I feel when I look at her. There is an unfamiliar pacing, shallowness, to my breath and although my breasts are still quite tiny, they strain against my training bra with a newfound fullness, akin to heaviness, it is startling to feel a weight to them of my own making. Blood flows downstairs. It's not a brazen blueness; it is enjoyable. Sometimes fear creeps in. It wouldn't do to get caught gazing ardently at the dancing woman's portrait; so when my nipples bunch and harden I stop. At the very least, I have the sense to know continuing down this path would not be considered good behaviour. I long to be allowed to read the books from these stacks; but my Mam says, when you're older, when you're older.

Our parents go on holiday and my sister is in charge. On those rainy Summer evenings, I finish the *Sweet Valley Highs* I spent the entire afternoon reading, she snaps them from my hands, ploughs through each one in under an hour then throws them over the back of her armchair, this is apparently hilarious. I ask her, will I be able to read as quickly as her when I'm older. Practice makes perfect, she retorts. I drive her mad looking for books of hers to read, trying hard to be let in to the coveted bedside stacks; she closes many doors in my face. I tell her I need to increase my reading speed for my Junior Cert, I'm really studying the art of reading. And, although I love, I am too old for *Heidi, Black Beauty, The Secret Garden. The Children of the Famine Trilogy* is for kids! I simply cannot read Enid Blyton, Paula Danziger, Anne Digby one more time. I'm exasperated by the foreignness of all-American teenagers. I'll be fourteen in a few weeks. Give me a break, please. She hands me three Danielle Steel books from my mother's stacks and says, there's no sex in these, it's skipped over, you have two days per book, read fast. I fling myself across the double bed, refuse to be beaten.

On her return, our Mam loses it when she sees the stack I've made of my own reading, I hear her nearly shouting at my sister, earwigging from the other side of my parents' bedroom door, hissing, there are erections in those books. Erections! She is too young to be reading about erections. She is just too young. WHAT ARE ERECTIONS?! How did I miss them? How can I find a way to read about them again? My sister comes into our bedroom and catches me not quite back on my bed. Rolls her eyes. Grabs a pile of books from a shelf inside her wardrobe. *The Country Girls* is on top. This one was banned, she says wearily, start here. She rolls her eyes again. Goes out into the back field for a cigarette.

My Mam brought me home some more Mildred D.

Taylor books from her trip. I thank her profusely, finish quickly and tell her all about them sitting on the kitchen table while she's chopping vegetables for dinner the last week of the holidays. My mother sighs deeply; resultantly I am allowed to read any of the Virago Classics on the bedroom floor! I ask her, is *Good Behaviour* even any good? She pulls a face, they're very posh and do not behave themselves at all. I now know whatever is in that book, it is not something she thinks I should ascribe to.

○

I miss a lot of school this academic year because my periods are near constant, crazy painful and extremely heavy. I struggle to keep up with homework, I spend a lot of afternoons on the sofa under my duvet watching shite daytime TV and children's cartoons. I bleed through Super Plus tampons, two pads and tracksuit bottoms. I have to place a navy bath towel under me on the sofa, and go to the toilet to change at least once an hour. My Mam drags me in and out to the GP's office, they tell me to eat apples and oranges daily and go for a thirty-minute walk each day after school. She slams drawers and presses shut in the kitchen those evenings. I am no longer a ghost me, I am translucent. My blue veined blood is tested constantly for anaemia and always comes back: borderline inconclusive. I do not sleep at all on heavy bleeding nights. The soaking is wholly discommodious. My mother nearly shouts at the GP, my education is important, I cannot be *in absentia* for all of Secondary. She doesn't mention she only got to attend Primary herself. I end up on the highest possible painkillers, and keep having to come home sick. It's obvious to the entire school I'm rarely off my rag. One day, I have to call my Mam from school reception when she's at her second job, cleaning offices once a week, I'm bawling crying with the agony, I don't say but—I am terrified—I think the whole bottom half of the insides of me are going to come out with the clots into my knickers. A male teacher says I cannot sit in reception doing nothing all afternoon and I am forced—petrified—to go back to my last lesson. I count the seconds until days' end all the while believing my lower organs are slowly coming away from me, layer by layer, into my seat in the middle of Civics. My Mam throws me into the GP's surgery. She is snarling that when they see me in this state, they are going to have to finally do something about it. The GP gives me my first of many morphine injections. These, I like. My Mam fumes at them, I will quite simply need to go on the pill. They say, it just is not permissible for a pubescent girl of my young age. We get home, she takes out the *Yellow Pages*, phones the *Well Woman Centre*. I'm not to tell anyone, none of my friends that we are going there; I get it—the need for secrecy— immediately, because I have never before seen her this seethingly angry.

○

Over the Easter holidays, Sarah, Tina and I lie about in her bedroom flicking through magazines. Tina is incredulous about a female genitalia diagram. It depicts three holes. She keeps reading the same bit out to us, there is the anus hole for excrement at the back, the vagina hole for discharge and periods in the middle, and the urethra, a tiny pinprick hole, for urine, towards the front. She didn't know there were two holes in your vulva, she never knew before this very minute. I am incredulous at her incredulity. Tina has had her periods since she was eleven! Even when I had the wrong coloured stain in my gusset I knew it was too far forward to be an actual shit stain, and I know I'm not wetting myself when I bleed. She keeps pointing at the diagram and telling us to look, just look at this revelation. I get quite irritated and tell her to, go inspect downstairs with a mirror in the bathroom; how does she insert tampons, anyway? She turns red and says, her Mum doesn't allow tampons. I feel I've opened a whole new can of worms.

o

Sarah is livid come late Spring when she uncovers Tina knew about my first period before her. I didn't tell Tina, my mother, not even my sister. Tina guessed later, so I assented. I still feel ashamed my body didn't do it right the first time, keeps doing periods wrong, and I feel sorry I didn't get to share it immediately, happily with my friends, my sister and my Mam. Sorry I couldn't make it more special for everyone else. Sorry menstruation has been such a full-blown disaster for me.

Instead of studying for my Summer exams—conceding already I am doomed to failure—I'm re-reading a Young Adult book bought second-hand in *Chapters* after one of our now regular visits to the *Well Woman Clinic* where they are considering changing my pill. The female protagonist touches the spot below her hairs in bed at night. Not one of the teen magazines ever mentions female masturbation, I read about it initially in my sister's white with blue nude covered *Everywoman*. This academic year I've learned a new consciousness about the lower parts of myself, since last Summer's unmentionable sensations started, I try holding myself some nights to help me get to sleep. It is a restful space and I no longer mind touching myself, it's second nature to me now; even so I get to feeling like I'll always be on the periphery of normal looking in.

Regardless, I continue making my way through my Mam's stacks. One of the Virago women uses the word 'base'. I like this word. The base parts of myself. These base blue parts.

Purple With Mottled Black

You're in this massive shed. Or is it a warehouse? You see it has empty crates and *poitín*-looking ceramic brown and beige jugs. There's a smell of seaweed. You know the Kays have a fishing shed, this could be it. It's huge. And you had to climb up a ladder to get into it so you're like in the attic but the roof is arched. The ceiling has some kind of red. Paint? You think it smells of rust and you're studying it trying to work out if it's metal or painted wood. It's damp, you feel the chill. You're wearing tan leather ankle boots and realised when you were walking through the fields to get here that there's a gap in the underside of the sole of the left one for water to sneak through in a way that you don't know your sock is wet until it's already wringing.

The others are still standing near the doorframe. Some are smoking.

You pass by a cord for a bare-naked lightbulb to get pulled on, the door gets closed.

James calls out:

–*Let there be light.*

Meave goes –*Shhhh!* and Tomás give him a dig.

You walk towards the other end investigating the soon-to-be crime scene should youse be called in to the local Garda station to make a statement at a later date.

You hear Brigid going to Tomás –*Let's have at it.*

You look back. They hang over by the door and start shifting. You see them at it, and groan. Is this what stalking through those five fields in the half-dark has been about? For them to have the shift! Do they not have the shift every few hours like? And here you'd been thinking you all might be up to something fun—together—as a group.

Shauna starts getting the shift off of Robbie out of nowhere, over near Brigid and Tomás, so you tug the hair at the nape of your neck really sharp. Shauna's never once said to, or around, you that she even like likes Robbie. You were with him for a few weeks in the summer—but he was mad into like liking you—and you are not into being like liked by boys. At all. It's really fucking creepy when they like like you. They do go on like they kind of want to own you. And they do start making up rules for what you can do or say or think and seeing as you share none of the above with any of them you do think it's a mad cheek for them to want to control your thoughts they like don't even know you have.

You're four left and Meave and James are still up there, sitting on top of a crate, sharing a Marlboro Light. As if you all haven't just broken in here they're going to start a fecking fire now. Here we fecking go. Meave and James start the shift too, they've been together on and off since school started back in September.

It's just you and Dylan left.

And you are fuming. Thick. Thick. Thick. Thick.

You find a very big crate, and start rifling through it. There's loads of old rope in it. You finger the bristles and consider making a noose.

You and Dylan were seeing each other for six months in First Year and you really liked him. Particularly. Him.

Mainly because he wasn't interested in the talk, just in the shift, and you could do that. But, also, because he wasn't loud. Or fast. He was nice like, nice to your body. And not always asking you to talk. Then telling you what you said was wrong, or here's how to think that better; meaning here's how to think in his way. He broke up with you at the end of the school year via Meave. He didn't even tell you to your face – after six months of getting the shift off only you. You've no idea why. Maybe he wanted to free himself up for the summer discos with the Spanish students. He had fun after breaking up with you from what you saw, and what others rushed to tell you. Eventually, you were with Robbie, Dylan's best friend, for those few summer weeks, but he was way too intense for you. And you'd no intention of ending up pregnant at thirteen. So, you called that quits, well via Meave; because that's how it's done.

Brigid and Tomás have apparently stopped the shift because they call Dylan over.

The fuck!

And you know what's coming. Brigid:

–*Why aren't you with Cath?*

Oh. My. God. Please don't do this to me. Dylan says:

–*Fuck off.*

Look at the attic floor. Close your eyes really tight. Tomás:

–*Ah go on like…*

At least, at least you're quite a ways away. Dylan:

–*The fuck. Would you two shut up?*

You wish you couldn't hear them. Brigid:

–*Look she's just standing over there on her own.*

Could Brigid be making it any more obvious that you still like him? Please stop. Please. Dylan:

–Cut it out now.

So, he doesn't like you? Brigid:

–Well, I personally think it's mean of you. Really selfish.

Does she have no shame? Please, please stop Brigid. Tomás:

–Ah Dylan, would you not give her the shift like? Go on.

No. Stop. Please. Stop. Please. Dylan:

–Did I not tell youse to fuck off?

Your noose will be red with a blue trim.

The others have all stopped shifting now and are congregating around the closed door; around Dylan. James:

–Go on Dylan; don't be so selfish.

Everyone else is shifting. So youse will have to shift. Right? But, they aren't even trying to whisper. Fuck. You hate them. Hate them. Fuck! Dylan:

–Would youse not fuck off now.

Turn to look up at them all. Look at Meave. Meave taps James' arm. At least, at least she's on your side.

But then James goes to Dylan:

–There's no need for that.

Dylan sighs.

He actually sighs.

Then he says:

–I mean… she doesn't even talk to me…

Your bruise will be purple with mottled black.

Shauna is given the push by Robbie, she waltzes down to you and says:

–Will you be with Dylan?

You glare right at her.

–Will you?

Keep glaring. Whisper:

—He doesn't want to.

The blood will seep out ruby red onto your skin. Shauna flicks her hair back.

—You will or you won't, Cath?

You shrug.

—She says: YES!

And off she totters snickering. She really is a pain-in-the-hole.

Dylan walks down to you, and the two of you walk right down to the very far end of the attic together. You're glad to be out of earshot of the others. Humiliating? Much. By the time youse stop walking, the others are already back shifting, one of each pairing leaning up against their cold end wall, Dylan looks at you like he remembers.

—So ...?

He says. You don't react. He shrugs. He looks a bit thick. You roll your eyes and look away. He puts his hand out and grabs your face. Then he's on it. Kissing you.

And, it's nice. Kissing is nice. Kissing him is nice. Nice like you remember. And you want to feel something nice that isn't nooses or nothing or hair pulling. And he's the right height so there's no tippy toes or him stooping and just your chests meeting and your crotches yards apart which is mad awkward like. It's nice. You play with the curls in his hair at the back of his head like you used to and he's put his nice hand inside your pink and purple checked shirt and is running it up and down the edge of your waistline that's forming more into a curve now you've turned fourteen. And, it's nice. His hands are nice. Kissing is nice. When you're kissing him. He stops. Looks at you and says:

—So you want to be with me again now, Cath. Or what?

Look at him like: I never didn't want to be with you. You broke it off with me.

But you say, really snarky like *–You're one to talk.*

His face looks pained. Hurt. His eyes look darker brown, sad even. You've never seen him like this. His eyes go black.

–Well that is rich, Cath. Coming from you.

Oh. My. God. Why?! Why do you have to talk with boys? It does nothing. It ruins everything. Nobody ever says what they really mean, and you're not going to open yourself up to being known in that way. For what? The shift like? Youse are only fourteen – well he's fifteen now. And it's all only pretend going out anyway. You look at the side of his head. You say:

–Shit happened. It wasn't just me going off with Robbie. Be a bit fair like.

He kind of tilts his head, and looks at you differently. That look. The one you try to avoid. You both just kind of stand there for a while. Then he goes:

–Yeah. Well ... Look, I found it kind of hard to know where we stood. Sometimes ...

You think of dropping, freefalling through this attic ceiling. You think of your noose failing, the rope snapping, the impact, your limbs broken, your teeth smashed. You think of the pain. The relief. You think this is stupid. None of it means anything. This is why you don't talk to boys. Because like, feelings and shit.

You half-whisper *–Yes. Me too.*

And, studiously stare at the ground for a few minutes, so as to make him know the talking part is over now. You look up. You kiss him, once, quickly, on the lips. So, he kisses you back in return – in his nice kissing way. Youse keep on kissing. His breath gets hotter and faster on your cheekbone and he's biting a bit on your lips. It's nice, in a way, but it's rough, and there's not really enough space between your faces for you to get your own breaths out.

You take a step back and you're right up against the dank wall, and he presses his body right into yours. You can feel his hard on. It's a bit much. Already, like. Where is this going? You think of stepping out to the left. But he starts slowly kissing you with no tongue, and it's nice, kissing him is nice again. Nice like you remember.

He starts kissing your neck and you bend your head down sideways afraid he'll give you a hickey. He just moves to the other side then and you both play this wriggling game for a while. You'd forgotten he could be a little bit like this, now and then, too. In pushing back away from him you're only pushing yourself further into the wall.

Then he parts both your knees with his knee and has you kind of pinned to the curved attic wall. He's back on your face and gripping your arms by your side. You open your right eye and can kind of make out the others up there at their cold end all still going at it. You feel a bit too far away; alone. And you really don't know how you can break away from this, this—that they all got you into—that you agreed to; and because they're so far up the other end you can't just cough or back out nonchalantly, for a smoke like. Backing out now would be making a scene. And you wouldn't want to be a girl who makes a scene. Who wants to be that girl?

He starts rubbing both his nice hands up and down the front of your torso, then your chest. You're wearing a baby pink bodysuit that has tiny bumps dotted all over it so that Meave calls it your bubble-wrap top. The way the material is kind of a little knaggy and his hands are going at you isn't a nice feeling. You push back against him. Make a move to your right. He catches you at the top of your right arm and digs his thumb in. He drops his right hand to your jeans' buttons and twists two open. Shoves his whole nice hand down into your crotch. You freeze.

You think: Fuck! Fuck Fuck Fuck.

He presses his forehead against yours. You stand still. He starts kissing you again, really kissing you. Grown-up kissing. Hot and heavy kissing. Almost German porno kissing. His breath is ragged now, and the pressure of his face on your face is painful across your teeth and in your jawbones. You can't get your mouth free to speak. He, he doesn't want you to? He flips his hand up when it's right underneath you and starts yanking at your bodysuit crotch fasteners. Fuck. Shit. Fuck.

You push at his shoulders with your shoulders, and he negotiates his knee across the forefront of your leg— winching it in—his other leg on the far side of you. You drop your one freed arm, that somehow had got caught behind your back, and move it in to the tiny gap between youse, and start tugging at his belt. Trying to maybe create a space for some leverage. To shove him off you.

You think he must be wise to you; because he just pushes his crotch into you more.

You're scared.

He yanks your knickers to the side and shoves not one not two but three fingers up inside you and you twist with the pain.

You think—in these slow moments—if you stay still, if you keep kissing him back, it'll be over faster. And you're in it now. You like agreed to be in this? You agreed. You did. Didn't you? You're still sort of kissing him back. You're still. You're still; and you are kissing him too.

It's not nice anymore. Being with him is not nice. Not nice like you remembered.

It's sore. And dry. And painful.

He rubs his crotch against the inside of your thigh. Pressing and rubbing and biting at your lips. You taste blood. Yanking and grabbing and biting. You throb. Shoving and turning and biting. You tear. Slacken. And eventually he finishes. Ends. Stops.

Then he pulls each finger out one by one.

Moves off of you. Lets you go.

He kept his fingers in you for two hundred and sixty-eight seconds. You know this, because you'd started counting long since in your head. You look down at the ground, and start to do up all your outside buttons.

He kisses your cheek, and starts walking away.

You think of running like. But, to where?

He's off up at their cold end now smoking, and the others shout down to you that –*it's really fecking late,* and you'll all –*have to hurry back.* You wait until they've gone down the ladder, walk up, pull off the light, and step out backwards into the night.

Meave is all chat about school tomorrow and links your arm. The group slinks through the mucky fields together. You –*hmmn* and –*yeah* a lot to Meave. You chew the Opal Fruits she gives you.

Youse get to the crossroads. Shauna comes over and asks can she walk with you. And even though she's a pain-in-the-hole, and it'll take longer together; because it's pitch-dark out now you wouldn't leave to her walk home alone. You say *–Of course;* look over at the others to say *–goodbye,* they call or wave *–goodbye* back.

You do not make eye contact with Dylan. But, he comes over to you anyway, and kisses you a peck goodbye. He says:

–See you in school tomorrow. Break-time?

Do. Not. Be. A. Scene. Making. Girl.

You kiss his cheek and walk off.

You and Shauna start walking down the hill together. She links you, and you stupidly step deep into a puddle; more and more water seeps through your now destroyed and sopping left sock inside your tan leather ankle boot.

Shauna says:

—What did youse two get up to down the dark end of the shed, huh hun?

She nudges your side with her elbow. Under the orange streetlight she's smiling, tittering, blinking fast. Shauna is never serious.

You say:

–Nothing.

Hot Rocks

Her first boyfriend used to kiss her after coffee and oranges. It was a strange taste. But she got used to it. They'd sit behind the harbour wall smoking and supping vodka from a Coke bottle. Braced as they were from the breeze, he'd reach across while she was drinking and start opening her jeans with his free forefinger and thumb and she'd listen to people passing by above heading down to the rocks to toke with the others. Someone would have brought a ghetto blaster and she'd listen to the reggae bumping off the rocks. His hand would reach across to her belt buckle. She'd pass the bottle back. He'd have to take it with his free hand. He wasn't able to reach for the bottle and keep his smoke in the dark. Then he'd pass the bottle of Coke again and start threading the belt out of its teethed trap. She wouldn't lean back to make it easy for him. He'd just about get it out of the jagged bit when she'd tip him with the bottle again. She knew he knew why she was doing it.

He'd had patience. She gave him that.

Another tug and she'd be free of the belt.

She'd sit there dreaming up disasters on how to delay it. Fantasising about the sea rolling in next to the wall and the surf swallowing them up whole and lifting them off their perch. She'd hit a few rocks, crack a few ribs, and maybe break her face a bit too. But it'd be worth it to stop him. To stall him. To put it off, a long way down the shore and onto a crabbing boat that could inch and pinch its way way way out to sea. And they'd be like an owl and a pussycat going far from here.

She'd open up her cigarettes then and offer him one and he'd laugh and say he'd be as well to be breathing in air as to be breathing in Silk Cut. But he'd reach over and touch her hair to locate her face then draw his fingers down her cheeks until he'd get to her mouth and make a cup with his hands to shield her. She'd light up her smoke and he'd smile at her and she'd smile back and that would be their nice moment done and over with.

Then it'd be dark again and she could feel him near her but not close, and the hole in her throat would be opening into her chest and oozing down to the space where her organs once were, and she would feel hollow in the top half of herself and heavy as lead in the bottom; and maybe he'd smoke again too, and she'd sit there waiting on him. Then he'd scoop a well in the sand in which to place the Coke bottle and with his other hand he'd take her newly free hand and rest it on his inside right leg, and she'd leave it there and start counting to ten in her head forwards and then backwards in every language she knew. He'd move her hand until she was somewhere. She'd let him move it. And move it. Back and forward. Forward and back. She'd unscrunch her eyes and start counting the stars and thinking of distance and how something could be seen and yet untouchable and she'd imagine herself a million zillion light years away on an ocean of stars in the sky and how she'd like herself there and in that way and they'd keep going on like this over his clothes until he'd cough and sit up and turn his body over and away from her, and he'd do something she could not see and did not know if she wanted to either, making the slightest noise like he could be a distant star exploding in a galaxy light years from this one because he made it like he didn't want her to hear it but she always heard him make it just the same.

She'd still be aware of the music bouncing across the top of the rocks carrying clinking voices tinkling and saying what they'd dare and double-dare each other to do and no one would be listening to either of them down the back of the wall anyway.

Then he'd take a few moments and reach for his school bag and take out a Thermos of coffee and hand her a cupful and start peeling an orange and she'd suck on the segment once he gave it to her and they'd sip and suck and slurp on the sand until one of their friends shouted over the wall come if you're coming if you haven't come already. And they'd laugh, and he'd help her up and kiss her—his coffee and orange kiss—their only kiss of the evening. Then they'd make their way back to the rocks where the others would be and the radio would have eaten up all the batteries so someone with a voice would start singing their own song, and that'd be the best part of the night, and she would be relaxed with his arms around her and no hands to be watching out for, into the dark, until next time.

o

At summer's end when the night was still, and the moon was on her, she could feel him next to her watching her in a way she did not know she wanted to be watched. As he slid his hand over and undid her belt buckle, he could see if she moved or kept herself hunched making it harder for him.

So, she leant back slightly, and he kept on going, then he put his smoke out and put the Coke bottle away. He popped her button out with ease in the light and tugged her zip lower than she knew it could go. He placed two fingers under the fold and moved them left, then down and right. His hangnail was digging into her inner leg and it caught in the elastic line of her knickers that made her inside thigh red. She reached for his hand and tugged, pulling it up against his will into her mouth, taking the finger and biting the rough skin off. He looked at her with pure delight. Then he nestled his hand in the crook of her neck and wrote her name with his index finger in the joins of her collarbones and traced his full name down the centre of her breastbone and kept on going back to where he had been. And she let him. And the feeling of letting him was almost the feeling she had when she played a song on her guitar just right. The feeling of letting him was a feeling of letting herself, and himself, themselves go; and the let of it and the want of it kept giving her more happy feelings and she wanted them all over and around her. He had his hand back down where it should or shouldn't be and she knew what was next so in the moonlight with the waves washing she slid her jeans down to show her readiness and he moved his hand to hold the whole side of her arse and squeezed his fingers and she felt alive. And they moved back and he undid himself and in the undoing of himself she knew he soon would be undoing her and she wanted to be undone right there in that moment she wanted to be undone. He reached over and took the thing they needed to do this thing and put that thing on his thing and then his thing moved closer to her thing and they were made a new thing with both of their things.

Then he was looking at her like no one had ever looked at her, like looking at someone was something you so carefully did, as if looking at someone could be all you have to need or want to be. And she looking back and every part of her looking at him and him at her and this new thing that wasn't him or her but them, and she felt it. Love. And it didn't hurt like she'd thought it would, and she enjoyed it for the time it lasted, and at the end of it he put his hand back on her arse as it was before and pushed and breathed into her and she to him and then he did that little cough thing but louder and into her ear so she could hear it and it was their noise now for her to keep and they lay like that for a while.

Until it was time to be two separate things again and no longer him on top of her and her under him as a joined thing and they moved apart, and he slowly bent over and started taking off his shoes which she thought such an odd thing to do in that moment. And he rolled off his socks and jeans then his Adidas top and T-shirt all in one whoosh and he was standing before her near naked. He looked at her like she was special, then he raced to the shore and into the sea and she saw him there washing himself, and she was thinking what would he do with his boxer shorts all wet like that and she thought he'd probably throw them away. Then, she hunched herself back up with all her clothes back on and she looked and looked but couldn't see him anywhere. She let out one pealing scream hoping that he'd scream back. Nothing.

Then everyone came down to where they were, and they were all panicked looking at her and looking at the pile of clothes and asking her question after question after question. She knew they looked like people she knew and she wanted to tell them the answer but she couldn't find the way to make her mouth work that way to make the words and she realised that she couldn't tell them because it was then that she noticed her mouth was still opening and the scream she'd been screaming was still going and that was the noise in her ears and they knew then he was in the sea and they were running around frantic and someone was running up to a pub around the way that would still have a lock-in until now and maybe one person or two slapped her face very hard because it seemed to come at her from both sides at once and the noise stopped and the silence was infinitely worse.

o

And in the cooler nights they'd all still go down to the beach when in other years they wouldn't have bothered, and they kept going down there until the rain got too bad to be out to all hours and the cold took them back indoors. She would sit in their spot and no one would disturb her or talk to her and she loved them for knowing that she didn't want to talk but knowing too that she didn't want to be there on her own. And the music had changed from reggae to overtures and symphonies, and there was talk of starting a band with a maximum of ten members; because they weren't The Commitments but they didn't want to leave any fucker out. And the softer music it skimmed across the water, up the rocks and into her lap, and it warmed that place there where her soul now lived. And she'd join them when the singing started and she'd sit there toking on the smoke and being one part of a part of something more than one part less a part of nothing; and she knew at seventeen in this village she would always be that tragic loner girl, and she wanted to stay like this forever because it was her identity now. It had been the biggest thing to ever happen to her and the best and the worst and no one even knew what it was because there'd been no time to tell them, and she didn't think it right to bring it up after. And she loved that she had been offered this safe place in the life of the village that she could keep and wear like a raincoat and no one would be so unkind as to take it off and leave her standing in the rain underdressed, alone, and no one would expect anything more from her than to be delicate and shattered forever. And she wanted that feeling of belonging to never end, that people were nice to her and knew her name now when she'd always been floating halfway out to sea herself before this. She wanted to remember him forever because his was her identity now. So, she did, every morning, before half past seven, with coffee and oranges.

Hills Like Hemingway's

A Play in One Act

Dublin to Holyhead
Scene I

The waves across the Irish Sea are high and rough.

A woman sits alone at a table. Another woman stands at the bar peering into the bottom of her whiskey glass. A Young Woman and a man sit huddled in a dark corner of the ship, where the movies play. He holds her hand and draws circles round the edges of her palm with his thumb. A Girl, no more than nineteen, stands on the open decking, the wind hurtles around her. She peers over the railings' edge and steps up just one step, one rung. A Girl Child is on board with her parents. She is wan, not pale, more transparent in fact. Her hair is scraped back into a high ponytail. Her skin is so clean you could eat your dinner off her. But on closer look she's rubbed raw red. The bones of her skull are set so tight the skin pastes itself to them, she looks as though a roar of wind will break her. Or it already has, and she has been stuck back together with glue that has set down to the bones. There are other Irish women on board, alone, with friends, or one close friend, a partner, even a spouse. They are all on this ship. Not one of these women has a name.

The waves across the Irish Sea are high and rough. On that side there is no shelter, only shadow, and by this time the ferry is between here and high water. Close against that side of the channel is the cold shoulder of the homeland. The ship's windows, around the cabin, are made of mirrored glass to keep in reflections: it is just you looking back at you, and no one from outside seeing in, no one from inside seeing out.

The Lone Woman is in rich company. The Whiskey Woman is onto her second double, her third trip across these waters. He said it wouldn't happen this time, said he'd come back for her. She couldn't stay in the village like this, unwed. Her time for loving him is nearly up, she is hoping the whiskey will drown it. She's hoping to never have to make this journey again. He went back to America. Hard edges are blurring and she considers staying abroad. She cannot make the return journey again.

The couple are young and newly married. They have dreams of the life they will share, they have choices and always make theirs together, wherever one goes the other will be there.

The Girl has long since stopped dancing, there is no shore in sight. She holds fast to the barrier and juts herself forward, the rushing past so fast she feels slight.

The Girl Child's schoolbag, covered with hand-sewn patches of pop bands and butterflies, sits on the floor between her feet. Her Father and Mother are with her, sitting on the seats furthest away from other passengers. It is very cold and the ferry to Holyhead will port in forty minutes. It will stop at this port for ninety minutes then go back.

'What should we drink?' the Mother asks. She tugs up her scarf and is fidgeting with her gloves.

'It's pretty cold,' says the Father.

'Let's drink tea.'

'Three teas,' the Father says into the bar.

'Hot ones?' a woman asks from the back.

'Hah. Three hot ones.'

The Lone Woman notices particles of air all around her. The Whiskey Woman is sipping some warm amber water now, planning their new life abroad. She has a cousin who lives in Liverpool. She could take this money and set themselves up there. The happy couple are softly sleeping in the nooks and crooks of each other's arms; padded as they are from the elements, wrapped up in their cosy life's choices.

The Girl puts her two feet on the railings and rolls her jacket's lengthy zip to its bare end. Sticking it fast on the last tooth, feet up one rung, two, three, extends her face forward on the top rail. Pinches the zip's ends. Folds her jacket over, holds it up either side of her head. Monstrous wind rushes up in and around her, pummelling her to and fro as the engine shifts down gear.

The Girl Child is facing the emergency exit. She is biting her fingernails. They are bitten right down to the quick. They have rivulets of dry blood in the crevices—blood bruises—and fresh tears on old.

The Bar Woman brings three cups and a pot. She puts the pot and the cups on the table and looks at the Father and the Mother. The Girl Child is looking off at the crests of the waves. They are bright white with foam and the ferry is rocking from side to side.

'They look like white elephants,' she says.

'I've never seen one.' The Father drinks his tea.

'No, you wouldn't have,' the Mother says.

'I might have,' the Father says. 'Just because I say I wouldn't have, doesn't mean anything.'

The Lone Woman watches people talking. They have everything and nothing to say. The Lone Woman thinks how poetic the silence of noisiness is. It doesn't translate how she'd like it: *is fileata ciúnas fiosrachta, nó nach fileata ciúnas fiosrachta*. She searches for the right words.

The Whiskey Woman ponders, what if her cousin won't have them? What if they've no place to stay? She would have to work. She'd have to. She can't think of another way.

The sleeping couple are snoring softly.

The winds and waters roar. The Girl tumbles out her hair.

The Girl Child is an effigy of her former self.

The Mother says, 'We'll have two Irish coffees.'

'Can I have a taste? Ugh. It tastes like Whiskey.' The Girl Child puts the glass down.

'That's always the way,' the Mother says.

'Yes,' says the Girl Child. 'Everything tastes of Whiskey. Especially all the things you've waited so long for, like chocolate truffles.'

'Oh, don't start,' the Mother says.

'You started it,' the Girl Child says. 'I was being hilarious. I was having a grand time.'

'Well, let's try and have a grand time.'

'All right. I was trying. I said the waves looked like white elephants. Wasn't that smart?'

'That was smart, all right.'

The Girl Child looks out at the waves.

'They're lovely waves,' she says. 'They don't really look like white elephants. I just meant the foam like water gushing from their trunks.'

Nameless women and people travel undocumented seeking refuge and comfort abroad. Searching for shelter, safe haven, and some fundamental thing, something right. There are hosts of other people not on this ship. They are home, stuck where they don't want to be nor like. Few laundries left, they are outcast; or woollen *geansaí* to pull over for now, this month, next, two *geansaís* on top of their school uniforms, letting skirts out with safety pins, bobbins, elastic bands. Hiding in plain sight. Until the bleeding comes. Blood under bedsit doors and bathroom floors all across the lush and fertile green green green earth.

No matter how hard she tries to translate it, all the Lone Woman can hear is: *Ciúnas. Ciúnas. Ciúnas. Ciúnas. Ciúnas. Ciúnas. Ciúnas. Le do thoil.*

The Whiskey Woman stops her drinking. She has decided, if nothing else, she won't be going back.

The waking couple are rousing softly. They look to each other. And smile.

The Girl jumps, for joy and liberty.

None question their consent.

Scene II

Dad: It's really an awful simple operation, Pet. It's not really an operation at all.

The Girl Child looks at the floor the table legs rest on.

'Has no one said those daring. Kind eyes should be more learn'd?'

Girl Child: Then what will we do afterwards?

'Or warned you how despairing the moths are when they are burned.'

Dad: We'll all be fine afterwards. Just like we were before. It's the only thing that still bothers you. It's the only thing that could make you more unhappy.

Mam: I could have warned you, but you are young.

Girl Child: And you think then we'll be all right and be happy.

Dad: Well look, if you don't want to, you absolutely don't have to. I wouldn't have you do it if you didn't want to. But I know it's perfectly simple.

Mam: I could have warned you, but you are young.

Girl Child: I think it's the best thing to do. But I don't want to do it if Mam doesn't really want me to. And if I do it, you'll both be happy and things will be like they were and you'll love me?

Dad: We love you now. You know we love you.

Mam: I could have warned you, but you are young.

Girl Child: I know. But if I do it, then it will be nice again if I say things are like white elephants, and you'll like it?

Dad: We'll love it. We love it now, but I just can't think about it.

Mam: But I just can't think about it.

Girl Child: But I just can't think about it.

'I should have warned you, but you were still so very very young.'

The Girl Child stands up and walks to the end of the deck. Across, on the other side, are cliffs of stone and mountains behind the coast of the mainland. Far away, behind the mountains, is another other country. The shadow of a cloud moves across the coastline and she sees the mountains behind.

Girl Child: And we could have all this. And we could have everything and every day we make it more impossible.

'Suffer as your mother suffered.'

Mam: What did you say?

Girl Child: I said I could have everything.

'Suffer as your mother suffered.'

Mam: No, you can't.

Girl Child: I can have the whole world.

'Suffer as your mother suffered.'

Mam: No, you can't.

Girl Child: I can go everywhere.

'Suffer as your mother suffers.'

Mam: No, you can't. It isn't yours anymore.

'Suffer.'

Girl Child: It's ours.

'Suffer.'

Mam: No, it isn't. And once they take it away, you never get it back. You've got to realise.

'Suffer.'

Girl Child: (Holds head in hands.)

'I could have warned you, but you are young. So, we speak a different tongue.'

Girl Child: Would you please please please please please please please stop talking? I'll scream.

'*O you will take whatever's offered, And dream that all the world's a friend.*'

Girl Child: I feel fine.

'*Be as broken in the end.*'

Girl Child: There's nothing wrong with me.

'*But I am old and you are young.*'

Girl Child: I feel fine.

'*And I speak a barbarous tongue.*'

Curtain.

Pinna

When you would walk on the inside and she would walk on the outside because she was deaf in the one ear, and so your sense of balance grew in relation to whatever was on her side of you, and then it was too often disorientating in open spaces alone, where you would counterbalance wearing the outer edge of your sole down, and all the while trying not to keep thinking that you might topple over without the height of her always hearside of you, keeping its immeasurable watch out for your nadir, so that you could always locate yourself in relation to her stance and navigate the sloughing off of your inmost echoes pinging back from her orbit whispering, 'you are safe here, you are safe here, you are safe'; because who else could ever have heard you better speak stars talking into their wrong ear, all those times we took our luminous adolescent walls down in magnetic field studies of you, her; us.

Before Him

You think it's two, but it's only one a.m. You end up back at this house party in Ballyboughal. Ballyboughal! It's about as hick as it sounds. No reason to drive to it or through it unless you live there. Everyone is bolloxed drunk. Music goes on. Shouting and hollering for more drink. Bright blue plastic bags carried in from cars outside. See blurry. Feel dizzy. Try to look less available standing here on your own.

Think of how to angle your breasts. Check your cleavage-to-top ratio. You're wearing jeans, your arse looks good in them—so you've been told. Sit down on the arm of the sofa. Continue a little dizzy. Move further in so your back is leaning against the sofa's back, put your hands to your eyelids. The music shifts down a gear. Hoorah. Skins start coming out. Thank fuck for that. You really can't keep drinking. Music's getting good—so nineties grunge.

—*Heya Karen.*

It's Liam. Liam. You're sitting next to him. Shite.

Liam taps you on the knee, and passes you the smoke. Inhale. The smoke is good. You're fucking delighted. Toke.

Exhale. Deep slow breath. Liam:

—*Your man, Michael; not out tonight…?*

My man? Puh. My man… Think screaming. Roaring. Look pretty. Go to give Liam the smoke but he pushes it back to you. That's kind of not on, to be hogging the smoke. But you see another joint coming in the other direction so youse are grand like. Toke.

Liam starts drumming the beat of 'Heart-Shaped Box' on the arm of the sofa, and on your leg, your upper thigh. Jesus! You're practically sitting in his lap. Deep breath. Sit back up on the arm of the sofa properly. Fuck this impossible life.

Liam motions to you to move your head closer while he tilts his further back. For blow backs. You lean back. He moves in closer. Inhale into your mouth, a little further, hold it in your mouth and the very top of your throat, put both your hands either side of your cheeks, he does the same, move together. Exhale slowly into his mouth. Exhale. Exhale. Breathe it all out. Look at each other. You start laughing. He's laughing. Lie your head on the sofa. Youse're smiling. Slow smiles. He gets a lighter off Jane behind him. And you know you should like not be wanting to get seriously caked. Should. You know this impossible life. Well. But come on like, youse're just smoking. Not riding. Relax. Close your eyes. Liam tips your wrist.

—*Ready Karen*? Smile despite yourself.

—*Yeah, go on.*

Cup your face to his cupped face. Inhale. Take it all in. Lie back. Silly smile on your face. Feel good. Nice time. Lie there. Still.

Remember to remind yourself your man isn't here; and this might look really bad. To the lads like. Remind. Rewind. Remember. Your man? Excuse yourself.

Chill over at sound system with the others. Go to start talking to your best friend's, Aoibhinn's, older brother Lorcan who's doing the music.

A massive banging on the front door. Everyone hoots and acts the maggot. Calls for —*Ciúnas! Ciúnas le do thoil!* Silence. Door swings open. Lorcan shouts:

—*It's Michaaaaaaeeeelll!*
Everyone screams:
—*Michaaaeel!*
Act uninterested. Play hard to get. Wait for him to come to you. You know he doesn't like it when you act like you're his girlfriend. And you know what you pretend not to know, all about what he does be up to, on the nights the lads go out in Town. Hang back. Look pretty face. Talk to other girls and boys. A little. Not too much. Act available. Don't piss him off. Just enough to let him know you're worth talking to. You're worth talking to?

Liam comes over, crouches down and slips you the end of a joint. Say:

—*Thanks.*

He smiles. Saunters off. Turn your head. See Michael looking over at you, with unhappy face, almost angry face. You're. In. Trouble. Smoke joint anyway. Start rifling through CDs. Go to ask Lorcan is there any shoegaze? But, see Michael still looking over. Your way. Puh. Fuck. This. Impossible. Life. He's only possessive when it suits him. Feel a bit of a thick waiting for Michael to come over and talk to you. Feel like a hanger on. Feel a little pathetic. Feel like: why bother? Look back over; can't see him anymore. Need. Toilet. Ask the fella Paul whose parents' gaff it is:

—*Where's the jacks?* Because you're about to wet yourself.

Weave your way through the crowd in the sitting room, go around corner into the front hall and then up the far end to the bathroom. Liam and Michael are standing outside a bedroom. In conversation.

Kinda want to scoot back the way you came; but they've both seen you. Kind of smile and wave hello. Liam:

—Heya Karen.

Michael nods hello, with a thick head on him. Walk past them into bathroom. Overhear.

—Michael, this thing between you and Karen. Is it, you know…?

—Exclusive?

They just saw you. They both just fucking saw you. Walk. In. Here. They must know you can hear them. They know, they know you can hear them. Are they for fucking real? Want to leave. Want to go home. Want to pee. Want to listen more. Feel like dying. Liam:

—No, I thought I'd come to you Michael… I wanted to know… where we'd stand if I…

—Yeah? Hang on.

Michael coughs a loud cough. He knows you're listening. Fuck this shit. Lads do this?! Turn the tap on. Lads do this…? You didn't know lads did this. You had no idea; that Michael is your pimp, like.

Sit on the toilet to pee, before you explode. Think about your man. Michael.

His eyes. His eyes. On your face. His face. On the headrest. His face. On the pillow. His talk. In bed. His body. Up against a wall. His body. On the back seat. Your silences. On top of his. Your body. Underneath his. Your body. With his. His silences. Over you. Your sounds. Meet his. His cock. Your cunt. You. Two. Together. And over and over and over and he turns you over and over and over and over again.

Wipe yourself. Stand up. Flush toilet.

Watch your face in the mirror. Bite the inside of your cheek really hard. Hock red into the white sink. Take mouthwash down off shelf. Hold it in your mouth. Let it sting. Smart your eyes. Act vacant face. Act expressionless. Feel yourself beginning to lose it.

Die a little inside.

Wash hands.

Ear to bathroom door. Listen. Hear nothing.

Walk out of toilet. Michael and Liam are still there. Ugh! Look pretty pretty face. BE SEXY. Don't try so hard. Liam smiles.

–*Heya Karen.*

He's such a fucking stoner, can he not think of anything more to say like, than hello? Puh. Kind of look the other way down the hall, then turn to look at them and half-smile. Act straight face. Probably looks like worried face. Liam starts to walk towards you, and Michael looks at you then at him. You haven't a fucking clue what's going on. Act nothing face. Think you look rabbit caught in headlights. Michael looks at you like he doesn't give a shit, and just storms past youse.

Heart plummets. You are a bike?

See Liam. Still there. Looking at you. Looking at you.

He makes a move to touch you, and look at him. Think of saying: Did you just ask Michael could you get the ride off me? Just look at him. So. So. Slowly. Shake your head. Do. Not. Cry. Think of saying: I live in this body, all the days.

Walk away.

Die inside.

Liam calls to your back:

— *Pricktease!*

Ouch. That stings.

Ignore him.

Dig your nails into the fat pads in the palms of your hands. No screaming. Keep quiet. Be a good girl. Act nice girl. Step. NO. Spin around. Walk right back up to him. Stop and look at him. Just look at him. Say:

—*Do not. Do not ever speak to me like that. Again.*

Watch as his bravado crumbles. Nod your head. Now walk away.

Walk. Sitting room. Michael standing with a group of lads. See him seeing you, then ignoring you. As fucking usual. FUCK HIM! Yeah, fuck him, right? Pass by. Michael reaches and grabs your wrist from behind. Down low. Out of sight. Tugs you back. Stand apart. Wait there. Still. You, a statue. Lads are talking. Words. Remember to breathe. Ignore your body's readiness. Ignore yourself swelling with the need of him. Your every nerve-ending ready with this hardest want to clusterfuck your life up. Go there. But you just can't lift your eyes to meet those, his eyes. Don't go there. Your bodies inches apart. Go there. He puts his hand at the back of your hip where your top doesn't quite meet your jeans. Don't go there. Rubs his thumb on your bare skin. Go there. Where no one else can see he's doing that. Don't go there. Standing almost next to you, behind you. He tugs on your top. Leaves. Which means follow him. As you round the corner into the hall he holds your hand.

Hold hands. Act needless. Be low-maintenance. Lads want that.

He finds an empty bedroom. Follow inside. He closes the door over your shoulder. KISS. Kiss a lot. Kiss with tongues. Keep kissing. Kiss against the door. Turn each other round. And round. You against the wall. Him against the door. And round. Wall. Door. Wall. Door. Round. Round. Round. Kiss. Kiss. Kiss. Kiss. Kissing. Kissing like riding. Kissing like you want to be inside each other's bodies. Kissing as consummation. Kiss. Kiss until your kissing gets too hot. Stop. Both stop. Must stop. If only, if only he wasn't so good at it. If only you weren't this good. Together. If only. He looks at you, then kisses your forehead lovingly. Kicks off his runners, goes over turns on the bedside light. Starts talking:

—*Never thought I'd get out tonight. Had an assignment to finish.*

Now he's all chat with you.

—*Oh, right.*

—*I could not get it done. Only finished at midnight.*

Telling you about his day.

—*That's rough.*

—*Have to write a presentation on it tomorrow. You're not working, right?*

Asking you about yours.

—*Not this weekend.*

Why does he want to know?

—*Will you be on email?*

For the online chats.

—*I can be.*

You are pathetic. You never say no to him.

—*That's great, babes. Can I email it to you after lunch for the once over?*

Babes. What are you? To him, with his *babes*?

One of many. Pin him down.

—*Yeah, okay. But, what time like?*

—*Around two-thirty?*

Puh. So say, to be awkward:

—*I'll go online between three and four.*

—*Great. Thanks, babes. I will too.*

You wonder if he ever notices any words you say. Him again:

—*I absolutely have to get it all done by dinnertime, because it's Lorcan's birthday drinks tomorrow night. Can't be missing that. You'll be there?*

It's not an invitation. For. Fuck's. Sake.

—*Well, Aoibhinn, you know...*

—*Of course. Cool.*

Whatthefuckever.

Motions to you to turn off the bedroom light. You are a good girl, you do as you're told. He's sitting sideways on the bed taking his shirt off, T-shirt on. He looks at you. Those eyes.

—*Karen.*

Your name is a statement. When you're alone together.

You go. You can't not go. If only you weren't this good. If only, if only he wasn't so good at it. What he lacks in girth he makes up for in technique, and it's not like with all the other boys; it's not dry or tight, stilted or discordant. If only youse weren't so good at it. Then you could stop. Could. You're standing there and he's taking your bootcut jeans off. Stepping you out of them, stiletto ankle boots still on and you're there before him—as he kneels down in front of you—in just boots, your knickers and top. Smooth. He's already touching you. Looking at you. Rubbing you. He loves this. Watching you being coy. He gets off on it. He loves you; shy girl. It's embarrassing being this exposed. He loves you; pink cheeks. He knows it's not the real you. And he likes to push you just that tiny bit further than you'd think you want to go. Your knickers tugged down he absolutely knows where everything is. There is no one else like him. You know. He's licking you out. If only he wasn't so good at this. So good. Other lads don't do this. So good. And if they do, they do not do it well. Too good. Almost there. He leans back. Standing, he reaches up to your face. He pulls you down, kisses your mouth. He's too good at it all; all of it. This thing between you will never end. You're both on the bed. Another lad would start riding. Not him. You know he's going to keep doing you with his mouth until you come. You lean into it. Further into him. Angle your hips. Spread your legs. You move with him. Into him. Into his mouth. Take him, his tongue further and further inside you. Dear. Sweet. Jesus. His sex could kill you. Resist. He slows down and his strokes are gentle, long. Resist. This. He moves up to your clit. Resist. His sex. His strokes are quick, quick; slow. Again. Again. Can't breathe. Don't want to. Resist. Your body moving into him. Circles. He circles you. Don't give it to him. And quicker and slower and harder and softer and circles you. His fingers inside you. Exactly there. Here. There. Everywhere. Hums. Can't waste this. You're moving. Always. Further into him. Riding it. Together. It comes. Up from inside and through the outside of you. Moving together. His pressure, your pressure. Releasing. —*O!* You see, feel purples, fuchsia, crimson, reds, orange, yellows. White. God. —*OH GOD!* Moving. MoveMoveMoveMove. Movements moving. Panting. OH JESUS! —*Jesus.* Fucked. Exhale. Slow breaths. Exhale. Calm down. Exhale. Out breaths. Exhales, slows down, while your body zing-zings on.

You're face to face.

—*Well, fuck me, Karen.*

You laugh. Happy feelings now. You hoist each other up to the top of the bed and rest on the pillows. You spot a used ashtray on the bedside table. Say:

—*Cigarette?*

You reach over him to get your handbag.

—*No. You go on.*

He doesn't really smoke. Say:

—*It was good for me, Michael. Was it good for you?*

You laugh, giggle.

—*Come here.*

He pulls your face to his. Kisses you. Looks in your eyes.

—*Fucking hell, Karen.*

Wink a very sultry wink at him.

Toe your boots and socks off over your edge of the bed.

You sit up smoking. Cross-legged. Place a pillow over your indecency. He lies there staring at you. Gently running his finger along your calf bone. Smiling. Watching you. Smoking. So you watch him back. Provocatively. For this time. Lean across him to put your smoke out. He pulls you back down. But you make it so youse're lying side by side. He takes his T-shirt off. Only notice that he's just in his boxers. You remember he has two hands. And, of course, he had a spare hand before. Glance down. He's still semi-hard. He props himself up, and watches you. For minutes. He slides his left hand inside your top, cups your breast, circles you with his thumb this time, and watches your face. No more shy girl, coyness, after all that, before. You watch him watching you. He keeps doing this to you. He doesn't stop. Won't. Can't. You're staring each other out. Youse're riding with your stares now.

You move to touch him. There.

Him:

—*Not yet.*

He gathers you to him in a way that you're lying with

your back against his chest. Nestled into him. He strokes your hair. Fondly. He kisses the top of your head. Sweetly. His erection fitted into the very curve of you. Neatly. Kissing the back of your neck. Tenderly. And your shoulder. Softly. You hate him like this, so you take your top off. He undoes your bra. Pulls you back in. He's really into lying there with you tonight, inside his arms. Cupping you. Stroking you. Petting you. Exposing you. Loving you. Not loving you. The sweet sweet hurt of it. Of him. Him.

You are so wet. You are always wet around him.

He says:

—*Karen, I came out without any yokes. Is that okay?*

No. HE didn't. Rage and fume silently. Why is every fella a bollix deep inside? Think of saying: NO. No! Pregnancy is not okay. Why would any fella ever even think to ask something so fucking thick?! For fuck's sake like. Calm. STDs. Calm down. Temper. Your temper. He is not exclusive. Calm. With you. Don't go off there. Calm down. Here. Exhale deliberately. Slowly.

Lie:

—*I missed a pill this week.*

— *...Okay. It's cool. Sure we don't have to tonight.*

Feel his erection shrinking in the back of you; his cold shower of pregnancy.

— *...I don't have any either, Michael.*

—*No. I forgot, Karen. You're fine.*

Feel a little—teeny tiny little bit—sorry for his blue balls.

— *...Are you sure? Do you want me to check the bathroom?*

—*We're cool, babe. Just to lie here. Come here to me.*

From babes to babe. Am I the only one now? You position yourself on his chest the way he likes you. Post coital. He

draws your leg across him. Youse're snuggling now. You
hate him like this. Him. Him. He goes:

—*We have time, it's not light yet.*

For fuck's sake, like.

He's only ever yours in the weekend riding hours
between three and six a.m. And you want him. Him. For
your very own; but no big romance like.

Half sit up. Tug at the duvet beneath youse, to move it so
you can get under, make a space between you for a time.
Michael goes:

—*You cold, babe?*

—*Hah. Yeah, that's the problem.*

He laughs too. You look right at him and kiss his lips.
Wrap yourself around him. Outside him. Before him. With
him. Him. He holds you too, in return.

After a good while, he goes:

—*Heya. I need the jacks. Will I check for some yokes?*

—*Yeah, do.*

Because you want to exist inside him. All. The. Fucking.
Time. It is a want you can't control. Won't. Don't. He puts
his jeans on, and throws on his T-shirt. You lie there watching
him. And he's making faces at you. Salacious faces. Cheeky
faces. Mimicking your wink from before; but adding in a
hair flick. Youse're cracking the shits laughing. You:

—*Shhh! Shh.*

—*There's no point in being quiet now, Karen. Everyone already
heard you earlier. They heard you up there in The Naul.*

Flush in the early morning night. How very dare he. But, say:

—*Go on so, hear me again.*

Incorrigible, the two of youse, always with this minxing
about.

—*Stay there, Karen, right there, in that position. No moving. I'll be right back.*

You lie there on top of the covers, stretching out your limbs, tipping the headboard, curling your toes, arching your back. You won't be told. Roll over. Lie on your tummy. Adjust your breasts so it's comfortable. Tuck a pillow in between your shoulder and your head. Lie still.

The door bangs open and you jump up. But you're naked. Not your best move.

—*It's just fucking me, Karen.*

—*Fuck you. Michael. Fuck you.*

He tuts.

—*There you go again, babe, can't get enough.*

Shake your head. Roll your eyes. He kneels on the bed, holds out two closed fists, goes:

—*I got you a present.*

Scrunch up your nose.

—*Small present.*

He gives you a light dig. Opens his right hand. One condom, intact, in wrapper.

Youse move to get under the covers. You unzip his jeans, take them off. Take all his clothes off. He's naked too. The light is starting to come up outside. So, youse make a kind of tent with the covers. It's funny. Youse're are a bit nervous after all this build-up. You put your hands on him. Move his body to yours. Press the whole length of your naked self to his naked self. That delicious feeling of skin on skin. Move in. Move. All parts of youse touching. Swivel your hips. Once. Twice. Gyrate. He's hard again. Too easy. You take him in both your hands. Steady motion in grip. Run your thumb across the top of him. Circle his tip. A little wet. Too easy. Lads are just so easy.

He throws the covers back. Takes your face to his. Kissing you. And youse're going at it. At it.

Oh.

There's only one way for it to go. Slide your right hand under the pillow, put the condom in your mouth. Stop the other business. Bite. Open it. Take it out. Blow into it. Check it's the right way round. Roll it on. Stare him out of it. There's only one way for it to go now. You've started. Say:

—*Sit up.*

Michael looks at you, a bit surprised. You're not often like this. He goes:

—*Where d'you want me, Karen?*

—*Sit up. Against the headboard. I need a right angle.*

He makes a surprised face, it's also a yeah-I'm-already-moving face. Youse only really do it like this in the passenger seat of his car, but you both do have all your clothes still on then.

So, up he goes, and you straddle him. Kissing him. His face, his lips, his jawline. Run your hands through his hair. Kiss him. Tilt your head back. Kneel up. Your breasts in position with his mouth. He's nipping on you. Don't pull away. It feels great. You move up take him in your hand from behind, between your legs. Move. He's rock hard. Smooth the condom down. He goes to take himself, to guide himself in. Push his arm back, say: —*I've got this.* And lower yourself onto him, in one very slow, but fluid movement. He's opening you up and you are taking his sex inside you, from outside, to deep within, deep deep within. It's forming you, to his form. Youse're getting your shapes right. There. Savour this. Kiss. Start moving, rocking. Adjust at the front of you with your fingers, part your lips, so your clit is pressing on his pubic bone. Squeeze him, with your insides, so youse're tight there for him, there for you. Do it. Move up him, back down, slow. Up, down slow. Up, up, down slow. Up slow, down. Again. The other way. Again. Another way. Again. He's holding back. His hands steadying you both, either side, on the mattress. Straining. Go hard. Go fast. GO. Go. Go. Go. Go. Go. Go. Go. Headboard banging. Go. Go. Go. Go. Go. Go. Go. Headboard banging against the wall. Go. Go. Go. Go. Go. Go. Go. Oh. Headboard banging. Put your left hand on it to quiet it and your right hand on the wall. Go. Go. Go. Go. Go. Go. Go. Go. Go. Go. Go. Go. Go. Go. Oh. Michael's sucking on your breasts and you start to feel a strong triangle of sensations. Go. Go. Go. Say: —*Are you close?* He looks up at you from between your breasts. Go. Go. Go. Those eyes. Those intense eyes. Go. Go. Go. He smiles and says: —*Any minute now, Karen.* Go. Go. Go. You look at him with your own eyes and say: —*I'm close.* —*How close?* —*I'm close, Michael, I'm very very close.* Go. Go. Go. Go. Go. Go. Go. Then, you tip him on both shoulders, move him to sixty-five degrees, and you watch each other—locked eyes—and you ride up and down him three times; then one last time as you lower yourself, you smile and mouth: —*Now.* And slowly, as you both hit each spot on the way up, you squeeze the very width just below the tip of him, you make him come, up inside you, and it fills you up. You're full of him. And you are coming too over and outside of him coming, and you're both dying, living, together in these fine moments.

Two.

You both hold on, to each other, for a time.

He puts his hand down between youse to hold the condom while you slide off him. And you roll over curled on your side. He wraps himself around you and you both lie still.

After a good while, you've both been kind of drifting in and out of sleep in the early morning light, he stirs; whispers:

—*We'd better…*

And you start to crawl out from him, lean over the bed looking for your clothes. He goes:

—*Karen.*

You don't answer. Pick your clothes up off the floor.

—*Karen.*

Put your bra and top back on and scootch onto your back to negotiate your legs to get your knickers on.

—*Karen, look at me.*

You reef them up, snap them into place. You look over, kind of, still trying to avoid his gaze.

—*Karen, I just wanted to say…*

—*Don't.*

—*Karen.*

—*No.*

You grab your jeans and start whooshing them up. You turn to him, and say:

—*We're grand.*

—*Karen, don't be like how you always do be after.*

Ugh!

—*I'm not like any way…*

Stop. You lean over and kiss him. And he kisses you so good, and then you move away from him, sit on the edge of the bed putting your socks and boots back on and you look for your handbag, it's over the other side of the bed, on the floor, on his side, so you stand up, turn to him, say:

—*Could you give me my bag, please?*

—*KAREN.*

—*…What?*

—*Talk to me.*

—*We're grand, I'm grand. It's grand.*

—*Will you stop.*

—*Come on, Michael, let's go.*

—*Fuck sake, Karen. Tell me what you're thinking.*

—We… look… we can talk… again. Okay?

—No!

Shit.

—Karen, sit down.

Do as you're told.

—What.

—None of that, Karen.

—Look, Michael, it's after seven. We need to get going.

—No.

Shit. Shit. Shit.

Decide to stop being a wagon. Resign yourself to talking. Look at him. It's bright right here in his gaze. Act centre stage. Act spotlight. You're being watched.

—Karen, look, I'll pick you up later for Lorcan's party. We'll go together. Okay?

Shit. Fuck fuck fuck shit.

—I… I don't know…

He glares at you.

—Come on. What.

Not this. Not now. No.

—You're going to have to speak.

No. No. No.

—I want an answer.

Bright lights. Too bright.

—…It's just, look Michael, I, I won't even be home like… Look sure, I'll be down at Aoibhinn's and Lorcan's gaff before then anyway, and I'll be going with her, so…

—Well then, I'll collect you from there.

Blinding.

—…Yeah, look, I don't even know what everyone else's plans are yet, so…

—*Right.*

Long silence, and youse are just looking at each other not saying anything. Michael goes:

—*Karen, that stuff, with Liam earlier... I don't want it happening again.*

This is excruciatingly serious.

—*I didn't. I didn't do anything bad, Michael. We were just smoking. I wasn't like...*

—*No, Karen, I am not... I'm not blaming you at all.*

Oh, right. Say:

—*Okay.*

—*Liam knows we do be together. He was out of fucking line.*

Oh. Right.

—*I don't want it happening, so I'll pick you up from Lorcan and Aoibhinn's. We'll go together.*

Shit. You are completely unprepared for this. For him, like this. Can things not just stay how they are? You don't know, don't know how to do the next bit. You just can't. So you say:

—*Well, if you'll be there anyway for Lorcan like, that's grand.*

He looks at you like he's either going to hit you or shout at you. You wince; flinch. He looks appalled by your reaction. He goes very, very quietly:

—*What. The. Fuck. Is. Going. On. With. You. Karen.*

Don't cry. Don't cry. Don't cry. Don't cry. Don't cry. Don't cry. Don't cry.

—*I just, let's not. I mean, we'll, I want, I mean...*

Your voice is breaking.

—*Babe?*

And he puts his hand on your face. And you feel calm. And you manage not to cry. Barely. But he's waiting for an answer so you have to say something; in your quietest voice, with his hand still on your face:

—*I'll be there. You'll be there. Is that not... okay like?*

He looks very sad.

—*It is—just—okay.*

Shit.

You can't answer him.

You can't tell him. You can't say: I don't know how.

—*Karen, do you want to go with me, or not?*

I do want to, I do; but I can't. I can't go there, not with you. You'll, we'll, I'll fuck it up. I'll fuck it up. I don't want to fuck us up.

He's stroking your face. Go:

—*...Well, yeah...*

And here come the tears. Falling. Stop it. Don't cry. Stop it. Blink. Blink. Blink. You are being ridiculous. This is what you've wanted. This. Impossible. Life. Hold yourself together. He can see you, coming apart in his gaze.

—*Good.*

And he kisses you. Youse are kissing. Kissing. And he puts his hand in between your legs and is rubbing you, fast, hard, over your jeans. You're totally going to come again. This permanent state of arousal—need—you have for him, is utterly exhausting. Any minute now. Kiss him back savagely until you come. Come right there. Come in the palm of his hand.

These Young Things

—He hit you?

—That's how it ended. There was love at the start.

—Love?

—Or lust. Who can tell?

Their face freckled with late afternoon sun streaming through the stained-glass windows in Bewley's on Grafton Street. We used to get together for tea once a month, when we were just out of college, but with the work and the weave in the formative years of twenty-something life we'd missed many catch-ups. They were emigrating next week.

—You know the way lust shocks you? How you can want the body, but not the man inside it.

—No, I don't.

There was still so much I didn't know of that kind of thing; too busy socialising and working overtime in all the wrong places. I remembered how our meetings had always brought me back down to earth.

Three teapots littered our table. They always took their tea from two separately flavoured pots. One Lady Grey. One Earl Grey. Not alternating between them, but pouring both into the one cup. I swished my Irish Breakfast, and thought about how unrefined I was drinking a morning tea in the afternoon.

—There was all of the flirting. Holding my breath, tucking my tummy in as he walked past.

The tilting of your hips to angle your arse his way. Dancing past his office to pick scissors up off their hook. The tiptoes. The twist of your feet. The stretching at your desk. The arc of your neck. Sucking on your pen. The looking at him, being caught, looking away.

—Catching myself gazing out the bus window. Not reading my book. Just thinking. Of his hand on my thigh.

His hand on your wrist. His hand.

—And reading the same sentence twenty times a day.

—Wasn't he married?

—Separated. Acrimoniously so. There were three kids.

—Hmmn.

A woman—pushing eighty—clambered into the booth next to us.

—I bothered him. Too much. One weekday, I stared at him. I stared and stared at him.

He walked over to your desk. You looked at him. You looked at his shirt buttons. You looked at him. You looked at his belt buckle. You looked at him.

—And he said: 'You have got to stop doing that.'

Which meant—do it more.

—When did it start?

—Where all good lust stories start—Christmas party.

—Hah.

—Everyone was blotto. I'd given it my all for three months, which felt like six.

Turn in to me if you're going to turn, or walk away.

—And?

—He was all keys jangling in pocket: 'Leaving soon. Need a lift?' We took the lift, he jabbed the emergency stop, undid his fly; I gave him head. He dropped me home. After that it was all hand jobs in doorways and blow jobs in car parks. I even sucked him off once from under his desk. Cliché, much?

There was the weight of him, the heave of his heft against my backside in the shower. He had the richest smell about him—all cloves, no aftershave. He got on top of me in empty stairwells, leveraging his weight better. He liked the risk.

You were driven mad by those fingers; thick as Staedtlers. Those hands. You could really feel them gripping you, grappling with you, undoing you. With some men, you're not sure where they are. With him, you always knew. With hands that big there is no lightness of touch, that gruffness is purely sexual.

—Over time…

After the act.

—…we let our guards down.

—You make him sound great.

—He was. In many ways.

All of the sex, all of him, all of me.

You were delicious. You were decadent. You drank more. Smoked more. First pot; but not only. He got less eloquent, more haggard, keeping it all up. He slept more. Talked less. You listened harder—to nothing.

The sex remained. The sex got in me.

Having it. Having it often. Having it raw. Having it. How could you not have it? Those hands. Nothing left to corral you.

They scooted right. I could tell the small of their back had started to ache a little against the chair's grooved rim. They scooted left.

—You know, I'm still not getting the it-turned-to-shit bit.

—It was a long way in and it happened slowly. We were walking down the street and out of nowhere this kid on a racer comes zooming round a corner. Wallops me smack down into the road. The bike ends up on the tarmacadam. The child's left lying there on the path. And instead of checking on me, instead of helping the boy or grabbing the bike out of the route of oncoming traffic, himself starts giving the kid shit. Pure accident, and he's all: 'What the fuck did you do that for?' 'Be more fucking careful!' 'Don't you know better?' 'Look what you've done!'

You're trying to calm him down. And you're scrambling to drag the bike off the road before you end up with a car on top of you. You're checking with the boy if he's okay.

—The kid starts rolling his eyes and is all: 'Would you cut it out like, I didn't mean it.'

And he doesn't even ask the kid if he's okay, and he doesn't even ask the kid if he's okay; he doesn't even ask the kid if he's okay.

You're done waiting for it to kick off, so you walk on to get himself to come after you. He follows and rants on and on about how wrong the kid was and how right he is almost all the way to the pub.

—Then he says it: 'I'm going to say this. I never say it. But I'm going to say it.'

No, no, don't say it. Please, please don't say it.

—I fucking hate toerags.

Please, please don't say it.

—Scum.

—He didn't even ask the kid if he was okay?

And you're scraped and bruised and still no, how are you?

He is silent then, and now you wish he would keep talking, the silence is so big you can't ignore it; you don't answer it either.

—We get to the pub. I order a large—no, the largest— vodka tonic. I don't see him much for the rest of the night… I, I went home with him, though.

You have sex. You try to forget the words. You're in those hands.

—I can't… can't believe he said that.

You start thinking it was a dream. Like you got a knock on the head when you fell and imagined him saying it.

—He never said it again. Nothing like it.

So you think he mustn't really think it. He just said it once. But he wasn't drunk. Wasn't high. Why would he have said it sober? Why would he have said it at all?

—And you went off him from there?

Why did you say nothing?

—Not immediately, no.

They sigh, and look down at their lap.

—Then… well, then there was all of the recalculating.

Recalculating all of the fucking. There was so much fucking. You're talking minimum twice a night; and again in the mornings.

—There was so little time for real conversation.

So little time for humdrum monotony; and the talking that did happen was after, and in-between times, when everything is nice and everyone is happy.

—But, I thought on it all backwards. The grumpiness in the daytime.

The cheating he must have done on his wife.

—The complaining about traffic.

The tantrums over someone or something being late.

—Always being late himself.

Throwing his mobile phone at the wall because he'd had a shitty day. Kicking your stuff out of his way rather than picking it up. Never paying for anything, not that you wanted him to pay for you.

—And never paying for anything.

He got his drink. You got yours.

—Borrowing money not paying it back.

The €50 you waited on. Never saw again. The next €50.

—All that stuff.

The snarkiness. His temper.

The things unconnected to those hands. Those hands could unmake you.

—You know what? I think I've met him.

—Heh…

They arched their eyebrows. I knotted mine back. We carried this on for a few minutes each trying to outdo the other.

—…You did. We all have.

They looked at me in confidence; then shrugged.

—And there was another thing.

You feel stupid now that you talk on it.

—You know, wanton? stupid? …what's the difference, actually?

I blew out five increasingly slower puffs of hot air.

—I'd booked a weekend away. It was a logistical nightmare. Took so much effort that the lead up to it was entirely unenjoyable.

Perhaps that coloured your view on things. Blackened it.

The light had gone, and the old woman next to us was still sipping her tea; ours only dribbles in the bottom of our cups.

—Anyway, we were at the airport and this elderly man was struggling trying to get a gift off the top shelf. I saw himself walking towards me, and what did he do but ask the old man to get out of his way so he could manoeuvre his wheelie case past.

No offer of assistance. Nothing.

—It would have been so easy for him to—hardly a reach.
You saw it. You saw him. You saw him seeing it.

And I thought: I have no future with this man. I'm only in it for the sex, and his hands.

—Did you change how you were towards him then?

—I'd like to think I didn't. I'd like to think I was in for a penny, in for a pound. But, maybe I changed.

You did; you got tired.

They dared then to broach the elephant in the tea leaves.

—When did he hit you?

—By the end, all the time.

He beat your body with his body. He beat your reason with his irrationality. He beat you.

A long stretch of silence.

You think of him.

I think of him.

—He hit me. Yes. That's the most mundane part of our story.

He said something, you didn't agree. Backhander across the face.

—You know he's, he's knocked the strut right out of me. Don't know that I'll ever get it back.

Don't know if you want to either.

—Let's hope you will.

I roll my head nearly onto one shoulder.

—Maybe. Or maybe I'll walk differently now. Way way away from here.

Perching their head on their hands they watched me. I watched them. We watched each other for a long, long time.

Then the old woman sitting at the table next door reached across, rapped her knuckles on our tabletop, and announced to the cafeteria at large:

—No staying power, these young things.

The Perfect Flick

ENTER THE INSTITUTION AT EIGHTEEN YEARS AND THREE MONTHS. LEARN TO UNDER-ENUNCIATE YOUR CONSONANTS. START SAYING 'AITCH' INSTEAD OF 'HATE-CH'. WATCH YOUR MOUTH MOVING IN THE MIRROR. FOLLOW THE INSTITUTION'S STYLE MANUAL TO THE LETTER. SEE HOW GOOD POSH LOOKS ON YOU.

7.55 p.m. Make-up check. Foundation even and well-blended in. Chin and jawline: no visible streaked lines. Little shiny around the sides of nose: blot. Reapply lippy. Blusher: fine. Attempt to perfect eyeliner flick at side of right eye: fail.

THE INSTITUTION DOLES OUT LIFE SENTENCES ONLY. YOU WILL REMAIN HERE UNTIL YOU ARE SIXTY-FIVE. YOU WILL NOT PASS GO. THERE WILL BE NO LONG-SERVICE LEAVE. YOU WILL NOT COLLECT $200. THERE WILL BE NO TIME OFF FOR GOOD BEHAVIOUR.

8.01 p.m. Make-up check. Foundation: fine. Blusher: fine. Lippy: fine. Distracting imperfection on right eyeliner flick: fail.

EXERCISE IN THE FORECOURT OR DESIGNATED CELLS. EXERCISE WILL TAKE THE FORM OF FLAPPING YOUR JAW. BE AS SYCOPHANTIC AS POSSIBLE AT ALL TIMES. THIS WILL GARNER THE RESPECT OF YOUR PEERS.

8.29 p.m. We mingle and A talks of his upcoming research grant which has been delayed due to bureaucracy but is still, undoubtedly, in the works. He tells us about grant proposal minutiae, the redrafting process, crossing 't's and dotting 'i's. He should begin working on his project in earnest next term, all going well, and 'isn't that fantastic?'

'Yes,' I murmur, 'you are lucky to have this opportunity to spend your working day doing something that really piques your interest.' Everyone smiles and offers differing gestures of non-verbal agreement. A is pleased by my response and gives me a secret wink. He then asks B: 'How about you? Any interesting reads or writes lately?'

OLDER MALE INMATES MAY USE DIMINUTIVES TO ADDRESS YOU. THIS IS A COMPLIMENT. IT NOT AS COMPLIMENTARY AS WHEN THEY GRAZE YOUR BUTTOCKS WITH THEIR CROTCH WHEN SIDLING PAST YOU; FROTTAGE IS CONSIDERED A FAST TRACK TO MANAGEMENT.

8.58 p.m. Make-up check. Surreptitiously blot foundation at t-zone with tissue. Blusher: check. Lippy: reapply. Eyeliner flick at side of right eye still conspicuously imperfect: fail.

THE FIRST 20,000 WORK HOURS ARE UNPAID. SOCIAL ACTIVITIES ARE PART OF YOUR FREE WORK SCHEDULE. IF YOU ABSENT YOURSELF FROM SOCIAL ACTIVITIES YOU WILL NOT PROGRESS TO HIGHER LEVEL INSTITUTIONALISATION.

9.10 p.m. B starts in on a lengthy description of a journal article about 'Over-reliance on the PPP Technique in Adult Learning Environments' they are currently in the process of writing a read-response to. PPP—Presentation. Practice. Production. B clarifies that although the central argument was adequately addressed in the abstract there was a lack of cohesion in the conclusions that irked him days after having read it. The author had stated a need for a fundamental shift away from the PPP method of teaching; however, the alternate approaches listed seemed to echo too much of a communicative trend. B explains that if the author had noted the merits of communicativism while addressing the pitfalls of dependency on PPP, or any one technique, then they might have made a much clearer argument. But they basically, according to B, just poo-pooed the PPP method.

'The paper reeked of someone sounding rather unbalanced to say the least,' he chuckles. B feels the topic would have been better addressed if it had been written with more of a 'comment-tone'. 'That was their intended point, to my mind, but the conclusions were rushed for publication.' Someone flatters the speaker and all in the group are supportive verbally and non-verbally.

REPORT ANY DISSATISFACTION WITH YOUR WORK SERVICE TO THE INSTITUTIONAL PROGRAMMING MANAGER. THEY WILL NOT BE ABLE TO REASSIGN YOU TO ANOTHER WORK SERVICE. YOU ARE REQUIRED TO REMAIN IN YOUR DESIGNATED SPECIALISATION STREAM AND COMPLETE ALL WORK SERVICE HOURS FROM INSTITUTIONAL ENTRANCE TO EXIT. OTHERWISE YOU WILL NOT QUALIFY FOR FUNDING, ACCREDITATION OR FAVOURS.

9.49 p.m. Make-up check. Excuse myself—toilet. Foundation: lightly press whole face with paper towel. Reapply blusher: check. Extricate goop from corners of mouth. Apply lip balm. Remove all eye make-up. Start again. Eye-shadow base: done. Highlight along brow line: done. Add warmer colour to socket: done. Do eyeliner. Flick smudged on left side, thicker on right side. Wipe liner off with cosmetic wipe. Redo. Almost even. Fill in gaps. Flicks better. Not quite pointed enough. Head back.

SHIRKING OF SOCIAL ACTIVITIES WILL LEAD TO OSTRACISATION FROM YOUR WORK SERVICE. ALL INSTITUTEES WILL BE PEER-ASSESSED ON THEIR SOCIAL SKILLS. ASSESSMENTS MAY TAKE THE FORM OF AUDIO, VERBAL OR AUDIO-VISUAL ACCOUNTS ON YOUR PRESENTATION AND ACQUIESCENCE TO SENIORITY AT ANY GIVEN TIME. ASSOCIATING THIS BEHAVIOUR WITH BEING CONSTANTLY PRIMED TO BE COURTEOUS AFTER SOMEONE EJACULATES ON YOUR BODY WITHOUT PRIOR DISCUSSION OR CONSENT MAY BE HELPFUL IN COMPLETING ALL SOCIAL RESPONSIBILITIES OF THE INSTITUTION SUCCESSFULLY. WE HAVE PARTIALLY OUTSOURCED OVERSIGHT OF SOCIAL SKILLS TO GOOGLE GPS TECHNOLOGIES IN THIS REGARD. RUMOUR OF POOR ATTITUDE WILL ALSO BE TAKEN INTO ACCOUNT. AT TIMES THE GREEN LIGHT ON YOUR LAPTOP CAMERA MAY TURN ON, THIS IS AN INSTITUTIONAL GLITCH, PLEASE IGNORE. STORED DATA IS DUMPED DISCRIMINATELY AND WITH REGULARITY.

10.15 p.m. C sparks up a discussion on the government's current carbon taxation policy. I mention an article I read in *Newsweek* and everyone is duly impressed by my wit in recalling the non-biased views of the writer. People are really getting into the discussion on how monies spent in one arena cannot, therefore, be spent in another. There are a lot of contrary views on carbon tax and it is, at least, informative, if not particularly stimulating. L, M, N, O, P are guffawing at the narrow-mindedness of the taxation plan—'*economically speaking*'. Their politics are unmistakably reflected in their one-sided comments. D, E, F and X, Y, Z are impetuously jutting in and out of the main flow of discourse with their commonly held ideas and remarks, all the while leaking tributaries of a refreshing but pedestrian socialist persuasion. I watch them jostle exhaustingly for each other's attention and extricate myself from the conversation—jaded.

I nod in recognition that people have been speaking and I, duly, listening. Then, I make my way over to the next group where, in stark contrast to the previous topic, G and H stand having a most erroneous argument on the perils of organic weed killer. The level of paradox is not lost on me.

IT IS VITAL TO THE INSTITUTION'S LONGEVITY THAT EVERYONE BEHAVES AS SIMILARLY AS POSSIBLE. AFTER YOU HAVE PRACTISED UNDER-ENUNCIATING COMMON SINGLE CONSONANT SOUNDS AND CLUSTERS SUCCESSFULLY, PLEASE ENSURE COLLOQUIAL EXPRESSIONS SUCH AS 'YOUSE', 'AMN'T' AND THE FILLER WORD 'LIKE' ARE ERADICATED FROM YOUR VOCABULARY COMPLETELY. SENIOR INMATES

MAY SUBSTITUTE WORDS: 'CHERRY-PICKED' FOR 'EXCLUSIONARY', 'COMMENDATION' FOR 'PRIVATE MENTORING', 'PROMOTION' FOR 'FAVOUR'. IT MAY TAKE TIME TO LEARN THE LINGO. PLEASE TRY NOT TO WORRY. THIS IS AN ESSENTIAL PART OF TEAM BUILDING. WE ALL EXIT THE INSTITUTION WITH THE SAME REDUCTIVE VOCABULARY. THIS IS ALSO OUR WAY OF SELF-IDENTIFYING ON THE OUTSIDE.

10.35 p.m. Make-up check. Rub at blusher lightly with back of hand: so-so. Foundation: holding up. Pinch lips with teeth. Eyeliner flicks decidedly unpointed: 2–nil.

YOUR WORK WILL REMAIN THE PROPERTY OF THE INSTITUTION INDEFINITELY. TO BE CLEAR, INDEFINITELY MEANS EVEN AFTER YOU COMPLETE YOUR TIME WITH THE INSTITUTION. YOU WILL BE REQUIRED TO SIGN AN INTELLECTUAL PROPERTY WAIVER. THIS IS NON-NEGOTIABLE. AN INTELLECTUAL PROPERTY WAIVER IS NOT A NON-DISCLOSURE AGREEMENT. HOWEVER, UP-TO-DATE VERSIONS OF BOTH FORMS ARE READILY ACCESSIBLE AS PDFs ON THE INSTITUTION'S WEBSITE. IT IS INSTITUTIONAL GUIDANCE TO ALWAYS TRY TO KILL TWO BIRDS WITH ONE STONE.

10.37 p.m. H is a real flibbertigibbet and G is deadpan and sardonic. I am having quite a bit of difficulty and making concerted effort to understand this vaudeville skit I seem to have stumbled into. I begin to wonder if they are taking the proverbial when they both suddenly retire to the restroom.

Apparently not stage show, but showbiz enough for another few lines of cocaine.

AMPHETAMINES AND BENZODIAZEPINES ARE AVAILABLE TO INSITUTEES AT NO ADDITIONAL SURCHARGE. THEY ARE COVERED UNDER OUR GROUP MEDICAL INSURANCE FOR PRE-APPROVED EXAM ASSESSMENT PERIODS, INCLUDING SETTING AND MARKING PURPOSES. THE INSTITUTION DOES NOT CONSIDER IT NECESSARY FOR THEIR USAGE TO BE MUTUALLY EXCLUSIVE.

10.44 p.m. Make-up check. Add more lippy. Touch up powder. Blusher: acceptable. Eyeliner flicks unsalvageable atm: Waterloo.

ANY RESEARCH EXPENDITURE MUST BE REMITTED DIRECTLY TO THE INSTITUTION. FUNDING BOLSTERS THE INSTITUTION. SENIOR INMATES WILL BE REFERENCED ON ALL PUBLISHED RESEARCH DOCUMENTATION—FRONT PAGE, NAME AND TITLE ONLY. SENIOR INMATES WITH ONGOING PHYSICAL, VERBAL, ONLINE AND/OR SEXUAL HARRASSMENT CLAIMS ARE EXEMPT FROM RECEIPTING PURPOSES. THEY MUST BE IDENTIFIED ON YOUR FRONT PAGES AND IN YOUR ACKNOWLEDGEMENTS REGARDLESS. FAILURE TO DO SO WILL LEAD TO UNDISCLOSED CONSEQUENCES.

10.49 p.m. With somewhat comedic timing, J and K jump up from their seats and invite me to sit with them. I claim backache, perch my knee on the edge of a chair and lean my shoulder against the wall to join in their little chat. In any case, I have chosen a less than favourable position, by no means snug nor commodious, solely in the hope of extricating myself in less than thirty minutes.

I consider if they were flailing for decent company and ended up together? Now that I think on it, I often see them on campus sitting with each other. Do they spend all of their lunches, tea breaks and social gatherings wishing for other company? It could be they are happy to be socially awkward together, or perhaps not—but they certainly do feel it necessary to earnestly engage with colleagues and bolster each other up enough to do so. I have no idea of their sexual predilections, having spent little time in their company— just niceties on top of niceties. They may well be awkwardly comfortable. They resemble long-time lovers who have never had sex with the lights on their entire relationship. Simpatico is as simpatico does, I suppose.

CODES OF CONDUCT COME UNDER THE INSTITUTION'S ETHICS DEPARTMENT. THE TOP-LEVEL POST IS CURRENTLY ADVERTISED ON A ROLLING BASIS. POLICIES ARE SUBJECT TO CONTINUAL REVIEW. IT IS APPROPRIATE FOR VISITING RESEARCH SUPERVISORS AND EXTERNAL EXAMINERS TO MEET WITH DOCTORAL CANDIDATES CLOSER TO THEIR HOTELS. TAXI FARES, ASSOCIATED COSTS AND SUNDRY EXPENSES FOR THESE MEETINGS WILL BE COVERED BY THE INSTITUTION'S RESEARCH FUND. PLEASE DOWNLOAD FORM HB2738. SCAN AND ATTACH RECEIPTS AS PDFS.

11.09 p.m. Make-up check. Blusher: adequate. Touch tissue paper to face. Smooth on lip balm. Eyeliner flicks: Little Bighorn.

THROUGHOUT YOUR TIME WITH THE INSTITUTION YOUR SOCIAL MEDIA WILL BE MONITORED 365 FOR SUBVERSIVE BEHAVIOUR.

11.18 p.m. I glance over at Q, R, S and T, U, V hogging the best seats and the only table, as per usual. They frustrate me. I find their work to be substandard and frequently late. They spend their time organising fun activities to do outside work, never invite anyone else, and could be deemed the antithesis of team-builders; only they are a team themselves—a considerably fractioning team. I'm pretty certain they have all slept with each other, I mean successively with one another—via the grapevine, not just supposition. Two of them are known to prefer dating outside our department, but not far enough removed from the student body for my liking. They are through-and-through alumni, their entire university careers. I believe they consider research students and above, transgressions; and of age undergraduates, a silly pardonable guideline. Their flagrant selfishness aggravates me. I don't join them. They don't require company. They are so very much engaged in their own.

THE INSTITUTION'S MECHANISMS EXIST TO SHELVE ISSUES. WE ARE ENVIRONMENTALLY CONSCIOUS. WE ARE AIMING TO BE PAPER-FREE BY 2025. CONSIDER ANY COMPLAINTS ROUND-ROBIN IN FORM. BCC IS NOT APPLICABLE. THE SHARED DRIVE IS THE PREFERRED DRIVE.

11.25 p.m. Make-up check. Will do a little bit longer. Eyeliner flick failure: Charge of the Light Brigade.

WE HAVE NO POLICY ON SELF-FLAGGELATION.

11.36 p.m. Sighing, I scout around for another place of refuge.

INSTITUTIONAL CUTS MADE TO SOLES OF FEET AND/ OR CORNERS OF LIPS MAY AFFECT YOUR INSURANCE PREMIUMS.

11.48 p.m. Make-up check. Taper both eyeliner flicks with little fingers.

11.54 p.m. W prances in, a little sway in his gait, announces: 'Let's get this party started!'

POST-TRAUMA COUNSELLING WILL NOT BE COVERED ON OUR GROUP HEALTHCARE PLAN.

11.54 p.m. The slight /ʃ/ sound on the 'started' alerts me, and several others, to the fact W has been having a party-of-one-plus-brandy in his office before entering the fray... W went through a horrendous host of bereavements a few years ago and has since taken to self-medication. We all give the impression of admiring W's tenacity while excusing his below par behaviour. And, to be fair, he is a great brain and a gifted person. I believe it is a collective fear of mortality that lends itself to our silent assent of his propriety insufficiencies.

WHEN YOUR TIME IS UP YOU WILL BE NOTIFIED BY OBFUSCATION.

00.00 a.m. Clock chimes—and with his grand entrance, I make my subtle exit.

TURN IN ALL WORK PRODUCT AT THE FRONT DOOR.

00.02 a.m. Make-up check. Tip knuckles to t-zone and temples. Fixedly stare at face in mirror. Note many eyeliner-flicks' flaws. Rub and rub at cosmetics, smear them until they bleed.

Polluted Sex

Órla rocks on her heels tilting her uterus backwards in a toilet stall at Connolly Station. Puts a hand down her pants. Looks at her fingers. No red. Folds toilet paper into her knickers, thinks of how the fail-safe old-school way to stop most Irish fellas sleeping with you is to tell them you're on your period. They choose to stay far away from the reality of that, can't say they'll pull out covered in ripe blood. There's a certain kind of sanctity surrounding your menstrual flow, a hangover of old ilk connecting you to the tides and their transgenerational fears of moons and banshees. Most young fellas just won't do freaky, knowingly or with forewarning, worried it'll get out they're riding at all when they could conceivably still be set for the priesthood or denying the child's even theirs, *'Ma, I'm still a virgin.'*

And now Órla's got herself an English boyfriend. An Englishman, fresh off the boat, they're like heathens, they'd ride you ragged during your period, around the clock, have no shame about wanting to be inside you; but they won't ever do it outside. Irish fellas love the kink of the outdoors. They'd get up on you in alleyways, fields, the back windowsill behind the pub. Lack of foreplay is the major attraction. The odd Irish fella is wise to the moontime game and if you tell them you're on your yoke, they'll just keep pushing it in regardless, thinking it's your polite way of saying, 'I'm chaste.' When it's not. So, then you do have to say, 'The way you keep pushing your thing in is a bit painful like with the tampon already inside.' They'd stop tip-raping you then and probably look for a blow job for their troubles. Or you might get caught out, they might be like, 'Are you really?' and then you'd have to say something small and feeble like, 'Why would I lie?' But maybe, maybe it's just the almost-men Órla's known. She washes then shakes her hands splashing the mirrored sink.

So, Órla got herself an English boyfriend, to piss her Da off. Specifically one who actively seeks to robustly discuss an Irish take on The Troubles, to piss her cousin, Senán, off. The English boyfriend dutifully tells his stock story about his earliest memory. The IRA bombings in London. In front of Republican friends. At family functions. And how he was with his parents and his father was pulling him by the right hand, really hard, and all he remembers to this day is the blood. It shuts everyone up. Blood on the newspapers, on the city centre pavement. Órla likes watching her Da squirm. And how red it was. Watching Senán's colour rise. And how that is his earliest memory. They can't deny an Englishman his own childhood. And how he'll never forget it. She loves watching the Irishmen stuck, gulping their pints, in pregnant rage. Her fella's story seems to Órla like an incredibly sexy earliest memory. Like, really, her fella's actual earliest memory was playing with Lego or eating apple tart; but the London Bombings were just too fucking sexy to leave out of any given conversation.

And yeah, Órla's well aware she's a bit of a cunt too, herself like. Growing up, watching the main evening news and waiting for it: 'A person was killed today, a Catholic.' Then: 'A person was killed today, a Protestant.' That's how you knew the news was over, the religious always died at the end.

She's standing in the main concourse at Connolly Station. Órla approaches the platform display, trains heading both north and south, she grimaces passing beneath.

Funny how it was the English boyfriend who first told her that her own father had missed being blown up in the Dublin-Monaghan bombings by only a few minutes. Wondering now if any of those *Iarnród Éireann* bomb threats of her youth were ever real bombs and never once thinking there was an actual bomb. Her warped immunity in the Republic of Ireland.

But now, now the Omagh bombing has hit her hard. Newsreel playing, brain cogs spinning. Safety concerns aren't all the way up there anymore but down here and getting closer. Being haunted by the woman pregnant with twins. Twins. The Spanish woman. The schoolboys. Boys. Learning how people were corralled into the street for the boom. Blood on all the newsreels of Market Street pavements. And how red it was. All that death in her face blasting across the TV. Blaring from people's mouths on all sides. And how the dead populate her short-term memory now. Like everyone else just seems to be able to get on with it while she spends her days freaking-the-fuck-out.

Órla's walking north through Connolly Station to the Dublin–Belfast trainline, fluorescent underpass lights thrumming through her head, each and every footstep flooding her ears. Newsreel playing, brain cogs spinning. Clenching muscles tight and then releasing. Waiting on the blood. Toilet paper in her knickers. Thinking about the blood. Stemming the flow. Up and out to yellow paint scrawled across brickwork: *Fan taobh thiar den líne seo.*

Rachel's waiting on platform seven, her train already in from Maynooth. They kiss, a peck, on the lips in broad daylight. Hug like girls hug girls. Hold hands like young women can and do. Rachel:

'Text my Dad we're on our way, I've no credit.'

Órla pulls her phone from her bag and turns it on, it beeps again and again and again... Six messages from Barry's number:

U on ur way 2 d sticks?

HRH lookin u

HRH drinkin my cofffffeeeeee

HRH lookin fine in his boxers

HRH watchin cd:uk w/ me

HRH still here

In d flat like?

yeaaaah

tell him am gone home for wkend

U left him sleepin in bed. Cut him loose alrdy

go fuck urself Bar

wudn't dat b a gr8 trick. Y u so mean 2 Duke of Windsor

w/ rachel. hes no invited

mind urself out dere. i hear dat's were d wild things grow

wilder u know xx

Rachel is tender draped around Órla on the edge of the train tracks. Órla powers her phone back off. She knows two things. One: kissing girls is nicer than kissing boys. Tastes nicer, feels softer, more receptive, interactive. And the feeling builds. Like you're really there with her, the girl. Like someone is kissing you and you are kissing them. You really know one another. Órla likes kissing girls. Órla likes kissing Rachel. Two: she's not gay. Because you'd know if you were gay, like.

o

Slouched over Órla, both of them taking up four seats on the train, legs splayed over duffel bags, feet resting on seat rims opposite, Rachel's demolishing a packet of crisps. Órla:

'Healthy breakfast.'

'It's nearly lunchtime.'

'The absolute stink of them.'

Rachel leans over, bites Órla's earlobe.

'Monster Munch.'

Órla laughs.

'Would you fuck off.'

Rachel breathes onto Órla's face.

'Cow.'

Órla grabs the packet, jumps up and tussles with her, pretending to throw them out the window. Rachel's right up in Órla's space now and the train is going *ckckck-ckckck-ckckck-ckckck-ckckck-ckckck-ckckck-ckckck-ckckck*. Thrumming noise and motion increasing. *Ckckck-ckckck-ckckck*. Clenching muscles tight and then releasing. *Ckckck-ckckck-ckckck*. Blood-filled images spilling, spooling, haunting. *Ckckck-ckckck-ckckck*. Light and dark spinning, flooding. *Ckckck-ckckck-ckck—*

Rocked by the Enterprise from Belfast hurtling in the other direction. Screeching, blasting, blaring bombards her skull. Tightness darts her chest. Sharp pains. Skipped heartbeats. Órla rocks backwards; then sits and tosses Rachel her crisps. Rachel:

'What's…'

'Nothing, nothing.'

'Is it the train thing?'

'Yeh, I just, can't…'

'S'okay to be nervous sometimes, petal.'

'I just, I…'

'S'okay.'

Rachel turns on her discman, gives Órla one earbud, throws her coat over the two of them and they snuggle, heads resting on heads. Hands held under their makeshift blanket. Every time the bell sounds for a station announcement Órla gives a little jolt, then Rachel touches and presses Órla's palm heart flesh with her thumb. They doze. Rachel shifts and kisses Órla on the collarbone. Órla:

'Next stop?'

'Next to nothing.'

It's always funny, Órla always laughs. She stretches her arms out to touch her toes, yanks the earbud out of Rachel's ear. Rachel:

'Heya! Watch it.'

'Hah.'

'Are you coming to mine and on to the pub from there, or heading to yours first or what?'

'Yours and pub. I'll go home in the morning.'

'Snaking about the town like you're not from here.'

'Pretty much… Sure would you look at your one who's

long finished in Maynooth and won't move home talking; but like, it's just too much hassle, we'd be dead late out.'

'I have a job.'

'Please. You're no better than me.'

'If you think so.'

Rachel rolls her eyes, lobs Órla her knapsack and hoots off the train. Órla puts one bag on each shoulder, bundles up their coats, chases after her. Catches Rachel by her rear pocket before she goes through the turnstile.

'Thanks for being kind about the noise.'

Then Órla grabs Rachel in a headlock and kisses the parting in her hair with a resounding smack. Rachel's dad beeps the car horn at them and they run over, both piling onto the back seat.

o

Rachel carries two cups of coffee—spiked with Tia Maria— and settles next to Órla on the bed. Rachel's skin is still damp from her shower. Órla thinks it smells of Palmolive and sugar. Órla licks Rachel's shoulder. Rachel kisses her full blown on the mouth, parting Órla's lips with her tongue. Folding into her is sweetening, fast and still. The immediacy of wetness surprises. Órla backs up. Rachel:

'What?'

'I'm waiting on the blood. I think it just came.'

'I'm glad something came.'

'Get fucked.'

'Again. Too easy.'

Rachel pulls a tampon from the bedside drawer and sips the now lukewarm poor woman's Irish coffee, lets her bath towel fall and Órla stares at her flawless in the lamplight in her pelt. Órla:

'I have to go the loo.'

'I'm giving you my towel.'

o

There's no toilet roll and Órla rocks on her heels tilting her uterus backwards. Puts her hand down her pants, looks at her fingers. No red. Opens the linen cupboard, tears then folds kitchen paper into her knickers and washes her hands in the bathroom sink with Fairy Liquid. Órla crosses back the hall, squinting in at Rachel through a gap in the door. Órla murmurs:

'There's nothing to wash with in the bathroom.'

'My dad can't shop for shite on his own. Hang on.'

They go into the bathroom, Rachel motions to the bar of soap and Órla says: 'False alarm.'

Rachel turns on the shower:

'Okay.'

Órla strips off and nods at the tampon:

'No, false alarm.'

'I can't get in with you.'

'You can watch me though.'

Órla uses a hotel-sized shampoo, starts washing her pubic hair. Rachel laughs:

'Are you going to condition?'

'It's hair, why would you use soap?'

Órla lathers her body in Palmolive, rinses it all off. Takes the showerhead from its cradle and starts soaking upwards between her legs. Rachel groans and touches herself. Órla:

'Come in.'

'No.'

Rachel sits on the closed toilet seat.

'Come in here with me.'

'No.'

The water pressure is waning, Órla adjusts the nozzle for a harder flow. She positions herself on the inner rim of the bathtub directly facing Rachel. Órla puts one hand behind herself on the wall tile and tilts her pelvis forward giving Rachel more of a view. Rachel stays seated, wanking. Órla bends her head, face to collarbone, stifling a scream. They both continue wanking. Flushed and wet she looks up at Rachel, who is smiling at her, happy and spent. The light flickers on and off.

'There'll be no hot water left. I've to shave for Saturday night Mass.'

'I was doing Órla's hair, Dad.'

They burst out laughing.

'We're finished now.'

Rachel wraps Órla in her towel.

'Turn the immersion back on for twenty minutes. I'm not made of money.' He chuckles and walks away.

o

Rachel: 'I'll nuke our coffees. Get fucking dressed. Or we'll be here 'til closing.'

Órla throws on an old denim shirt of Rachel's, ties it with a red silk scarf to make a waist and rummages through a laundry basket. Rachel:

'Do you've no clothes of your own?'

'I was going to ask for your big hoop earrings too.'

'Headwrecker.'

'I don't need a tampon but do you've any liners?'

'Yeah, here. Is it tights you're after?'

'Tights, and a sickly condensed milk kiss.'

'Top of the range that Tia Maria coffee, top of the range that.'

Rachel pulls a navy jumper dress from Órla's duffel bag. And they kiss there then, each in one another's clothes.

o

They head down to the beach car park with a six-pack and twenty Marlboro Lights, sit up on the boulders flicking lit matches into the night sky, watching them fall. Órla:

'You think we're getting too old for this?'

'I hope not.'

'Everyone else goes out for dinner and heads straight to the pub after.'

'But, they have job jobs and money to burn.'

'Credit cards, more like.'

'If we did that with them so little of the night would be just us together.'

'It'd be shite.'

'They talk about mortgages now, and Credit Union loans.'

'You really should start thinking about your career, you could get onto the property ladder with your qualifications.'

'And you wasting money on rent in town when you could be living back home saving for a deposit.'

'And her working in the offices in Maynooth but not doing a HDip, waste of a year.'

'Waste of four years.'

'Wastes of space.'

'Like we're twenty-six, not forty-six.'

'And we're all going skiing after Christmas, youse should come.'

'Skiing!'

'Who from round here has ever gone skiing before now.'

'But we buy the suits in Penneys.'

'No, Guineys. They're like rompers for kids but we just get the largest size.'

'It's a bit of a contortionists' holiday.'

'Like magicians we stick it on the Visa.'

'At least they never make us pay for rounds.'

'The weekdays are so long without you.'

'Mine too.'

o

The pub is throng-full of people. Din.

Órla looks startled at first and motions she's heading straight outside, 'breathe' mouths Rachel and wrestles in between people five-deep at the bar. Órla is pushed along by bodies. Shouldered from one to another. Elbowed in the ribs.

Thrum.

Thrum thrum-thrum-thrumming.

The buzz of the human crowd sounds unnaturally like the thrumming of houseflies and dragonflies, mixed together, in flight.

Thrum.

Breaths stop and start. This racket. Thrum thrum. The noise commotion makes before it kills you. Breath. Stop. Yips and yells. Breath. Start. Thrum thrum. Breath. Thrum thrum. Stop. Start.

Thrumming. Thrum thrum thrum-thrum-thrumming

thrum-thrum-thrumming thrum-thrum-thrumming.

Ramping up. Clenching muscles tight and then releasing. Breath. Start. Thrum thrum. Breath. Stop. Arms and shoulders and elbows. Breath. Start. Thrum thrum. Breath. Stop. Start. Thrumming. Dismembered limbs twitching. Breath. Start. Thrumming. Breath. Stop. Fingers and hands and wrists touching. Breath. Start. Thrum Thrumming. Breath. Stop. Muscled forwards. Breath. Start. Thrum thrum-thrum-thrumming. Breath. Stopping.

Din in in in in in in in.

Órla propels herself into the beer garden, rocks and rests against the wall. Drinking air.

There are several old wooden barrels decorating the back. The courtyard is like a country and western set trying and failing not to look kitsch. Órla sees a spot near the space heater they could stand and have a shelf for their drinks. She jumps when a hand claps her on the shoulder—it's her cousin, Senán:

'There you are, back in the fold.'

'Hi.'

He passes her a joint.

'Home to see the mammy.'

'Just for the night, you know yourself.'

'Have you seen the brother, been wondering when he'll get here.'

'I'm with Rachel.'

'When are you not? Inhale on that, you're looking a bit shook.'

'I haven't been sleeping much the past weeks.'

'Bar work would have you like that.'

'No, I temp during the week now, I just do like functions the odd weekend.'

'I'd say it's good money.'

'It is what it is.'

'Are you okay, Órla? You look peaky.'

'I'm just not one for the crowds anymore, it does be like bedlam.'

'You'd prefer a quiet pint in Dublin.'

'Is a seat really too much to ask for?'

'No, you're dead right, dead right, it's not. Here, you keep hold of that, I'll nip to the bog, tell himself where I'm at.'

This is the village as a town now, joints flying around the back of the pub, Jägerbombs, rounds and rounds of double vodkas with Berocca and Red Bull, lines of coke in the toilets on weekend nights; flaunting the wealth. A schoolfriend hands her two pints and says:

'For you and Rachel.'

She turns to thank them properly and they're off encouraging a kid to scale the godawful-looking pergola. Rachel's waving over at her trapped in the doorway by some head talking shite.

And then Barry, Órla's flatmate Barry, pushes out from behind them.

'What the actual?'

'Órla, quick, His Royal Nibs is with me, he's getting a round in.'

'Here? Now?'

Órla feels faint.

'*Yes.*'

'God Almighty.'

Órla puts her fingers to her eyelids.

'No, no. Keep it together. Keep it together, pal.'

'Why? How?'

'He wouldn't arse off.'

'Ah! Fuck.'

'It'll be okay.'

'Will it, Barry? Will it be okay?'

'It will, it will.'

'I don't want this. I can't…'

Órla gulps air in. Barry lowers his face to hers and talks into her ear:

'Yeah, look, we played Nintendo for a few hours, he wasn't leaving the flat in case you came back, then he got bored or whatever and cajoled me to go for pints in some Republican pub near Smithfield, you know the way he's mad for all that, after those rounds I dare-made him go for a swift one in The George, and then he says, we'd get the train out here, there was no dissuading him, so I had to fucking come along; and he's fluthered. I've been ringing you all evening.'

'Mother of fucketyfuckfuck. Him and Rachel don't get along.'

'Ever wonder why?'

Órla bulges her eyes.

'Fuck.'

'Just drink your pint, you'll be grand.'

'If I don't fucking kill myself.'

'Grand, you'll be grand, grand, we'll be grand. Grand. Grand. It's all grand.'

'Stop it! Stop. Are you fucking high?'

Barry glances down.

'We did a bit on the train.'

'For fuck's sake, Bar.'

Órla dances in a temper. Rachel arrives and pulls the three of them together in a group hug, kisses Barry's cheek.

'My two favourite people.'

She puts two double vodkas and a can of Coke on the ledge, dumps ice into an empty pint glass. Starts pouring. Leaves a third of the vodka in the one glass, adds some Coke, swishes the rest of the Coke into the other glass, and somehow manages to pour half of its contents back inside the can; smiles, handing the Coke can to Barry. Rachel:

'Years of practice. Trapped by that eejit from my estate for a decade there, asking me about his sister's points for the Leaving. Like I'm the fucking CAO or something.'

'Rachel, he's here, he came with Barry.'

'Who? Not...'

'Yup, yup, him, HRH—I came up with that one, isn't it gas?'

'Barry. Shut up!'

'Ah now.'

'Sorry, sorry.'

Órla's cousin Senán and her English boyfriend, Mark, stagger across the back to them. Senán has about twenty drinks on a tray. Barry spots a vacant barrel with more space, motions to it. The lads bag it. Rachel, Órla and Barry walk over to them. Senán passes them shots:

'I found this West Brit at the bar.'

'Thoroughbred.'

Everyone laughs and downs the drinks. Mark clamps a hand on Órla's shoulder.

'I was missing you. You look lovely. New dress?'

'It's Rachel's.'

'Oh, yes, hello.'

Rachel, deadpan:

'Hiya.'

Senán is stacking the empties to one side. 'I was saying

before youse all got here, Órla looks a bit out of sorts.'

'It's just my period, okay.'

'Jesus, didn't know we were talking about rags down the pub. In fairness. Órla, we're family but we're not that close.'

Barry shouts: 'Enough. Let's drink!'

And they all do another shot. Mark still has his right hand clamped on Órla's shoulder and she doesn't know if it's to steady himself or to claim possession. Rachel's smiling at Barry—who's mock playing the drums—while at the same time she looks pure sad. Mark starts in:

'As a matter of fact…'

Rachel coughs:

'Oh here we go.'

'As a matter of fact, Órla's been a bit out of sorts since the bombing.'

'That is not pub conversation.' Rachel eyes Mark.

'It's something I noted. She hasn't been sleeping.'

'Is that true Órla?' Senán asks.

'Lookit, I'd rather talk about something else.'

'Something other than The Cause. Something more important.'

'I definitely didn't say that.'

'Well, I wouldn't want to hear something like that coming from a cousin of mine.'

'I didn't, I did not say it wasn't important, it's just like Rachel said, it's not pub conversation.'

Rachel smiles, properly this time. Mark keeps pushing:

'I've been trying to gather thoughts on it and no one has one, not one, one word to say.'

'Tell me you're not really MI6.' Barry is hopping about, doing 007 moves.

Senán nods at Barry, half-laughs; turns to eyeball Mark and states:

'When you come from a family like mine and Órla's you see the world differently. The Troubles are not separate. Not when you have skin in the game.'

Mark keeps pushing in regardless:

'Is that how you see it, Órla?'

'Ah, for fuck's sake,' Rachel mutters.

'Noted.'

Barry's jigging about on the spot; he goes:

'A drink for you, a drink for you, a drink for you, and you, and me.'

Órla's never loved him more than in this moment. Everyone's looking at her. Panic. Rising. Órla:

'It has had me upset. It's fair to have said that.'

'A little bit too real on the island?' Mark quips.

Rachel:

'For fuck's sake!'

'Again. Noted.'

Senán barks a cough, then says in a low whisper: 'You're not taking the other side, Órla. We'll have words.'

'Sexually transmitted colonialism would be gas,' Barry snorts.

Órla slams her glass down onto the barrel.

'No. Stop. Stop. Everyone stop!' Órla breathes.

Continues:

'It is upsetting when people die. Are killed.'

Mark raises his eyebrows, dryly: 'Upsetting?'

'I'm not finished!… But that is war, Mark, that is the harsh reality of war.'

Órla puts her fingers to her eyelids, exhales, then starts

tapping at her pockets searching for cigarettes. Her cousin passes her one. Rachel leans in to light it. Órla closes her eyes, sucks on the cigarette in gulps, creases then bows her forehead. Rachel openly glares at Mark, snaps:

'She's answered you now. You done.'

'Noted, I said.'

Órla shifts from under Mark's grasp.

'Don't talk to her like that.'

'Is that how it is, is it?'

'Ah here, mind yourselves, no need to get messy now,' Órla's cousin waves to some friends, who sidle over. Barry and one of the friends start mock ballet dancing in between everyone. Rachel turns to Senán:

'Fuck this for a Saturday night. You coming the jacks?'

'Yeah, yes, good idea. Look, you two, sort it out. It's everybody's weekend.'

Órla tries to catch Rachel by the cuff of her jumper dress. Misses. Rachel turns. Órla mouths, 'Don't,' Rachel shakes her head no. They go off to the toilets. Barry is dancing with a new partner now and old schoolfriends are jostling, curtseying and pirouetting. Everyone is having a flying night. Órla faces Mark.

'Can you never just leave it for one minute?'

Mark props himself up against the wall.

'I'm interested in current events.'

Órla takes one step towards him. Waits.

Mark:

'Sue me.'

Órla looks at him. Disgusted.

'We are not a fucking ethnographical study.'

Mark blinks. Fast.

'I'm interested in you.'

He tries to touch her face. Órla backs away.

'It's not okay. Following me. Bossing me in public.'

Mark downs the end of someone's flat pint, says:

'Sorry.'

'Sorry.'

'Can we just…'

He's reaching, trying to grab Órla's hands but he keeps missing. So he's just grabbing at her. Órla pushes him back up to standing height against the wall, leans into his ear, pleads:

'Mark, she's my best friend.'

'Is that what she is. Is she?'

The house lights go on inside.

Almost the entire pub is congregating out the back now.

The first bars of *Amhrán na bhFiann* start up through the loudspeakers.

Órla chokes:

'It's fucking suffocating here.'

She walks away.

A widening circle is forming.

Barry takes her by the waist, stretches his arm out, Órla clasps his hand and he dances her along the inner edge. They are standing at the cigarette machine next to the back door while the last few stragglers head outside to take part in the upcoming rounds of rebel songs.

When the national anthem is over, Barry starts emptying his pockets into the slot, Órla hands him what's left of her loose change. He hits every button until they end up with a packet of Benson & Hedges. They stand in the doorway, looking at the congregation, enveloped in harsh-tasting tar and regrets.

Barry works on rolling some mini-joints for later. Órla says:

'Do you ever see music, like the notes appearing above people's heads, while a song is being sung, and how they might drift off or break away when there is an echo of discord, dissonance, and you fix your eyes on it, willing it to stop drifting, sending it some kind of energy, to forget the slip, to just float back down, rejoin the chorus, but it can't; it's happened, there's this brokenness, a jagged bit, that'll always be outside of the circle. And you, you both know this, but you keep fixed on it, willing it, to fit back in.'

Barry takes her lit cigarette with a mile of ash balanced off its end, carefully, then flicks the underside of it with his middle finger. The ash falls onto the courtyard.

'You'll have to choose.'

He tilts her face, he kisses her temple. Órla:

'I have to be just one thing.'

'This, you know this…' Barry gestures, 'it's, it's not kind.'

Órla doubles over, and he can tell she is crying.

'I think I'm going to be sick.'

o

Standing at the sink Órla knows she should probably make herself throw up, but she also thinks about what a desperate waste of money that would be, so doesn't. She slides her hand into her pants, feels for the blood, nothing, rocks backwards on her heels and rests her head against the tiled wall. She considers having a wank, because anything, literally anything, would be better than this. There's squeaking and scraping coming from the other side. She knocks, four taps. Someone knocks four taps back. She knocks six taps. Someone knocks six taps back. She knocks again. Someone knocks back, waits, another, waits, then another, waits, then another, waits, then another, until there's just palms banging and banging on the wall. She walks out and opens the door to a storeroom. Senán and Rachel are standing there drumming their fingers, slapping and chasing each other's hands up the walls. Walls that are covered in game upon game of Xs and Os, game upon game upon game of Xs and Os decorate the storeroom walls. Órla:

'What the— what in the actual name of fuck are youse two doing?'

'We found a pen,' Órla's cousin laughs. Rachel:

'It started with best of three.'

They break their shits laughing. Órla shakes her head at them.

'We'll never be let in here again.'

Rachel looks at her.

'Unlikely,' she scoffs.

Senán shrugs: 'They've started cleaning the front bar, so we thought we'd hide in here to do a bit.'

'A lot.'

'A lot of a bit.'

'Of a bit of a lot.'

Órla is visibly pissed off. 'Drinking up time's almost over. Come on, let's go.' Rachel:

'But we can't remember who's winning.'

Órla, half to herself:

'Time. Time is always fucking winning.'

Órla pulls them both out of the storeroom and hands them a mini-joint from the inner lining of her handbag.

'Here, get started on some of this, then we'll go. Absolute state of youse two.'

She's that kind of angry-sad where you don't know if someone is fuming or near devastated. Senán:

'She's getting very judgemental in her old age.'

Rachel shakes her head, 'Very very judgemental.'

Órla spits at her cousin:

'Inhale. You look a bit shook.'

'Trying to be funny there cos I said that to her earlier.'

'Funny,' Rachel snickers.

'Funny,' Senán smirks.

'Funny,' Órla tuts.

'Where are we heading to after?'

'I'd say that's getting decided now. Will you go check?' Órla asks Senán. Senán:

'Did you sort it out? Is the row over?'

'It is what it is.'

'Órla, look, I'll say this to you because we're family and please, I'm being dead serious now, so don't get me wrong; it's not just because he's English. And I mean that. I really do. But, Órla, he is dry as shite.'

Rachel raises her right hand and Senán gives her a high five, then he walks off.

Órla:

'Rachel, can we please go?'

'Where?'

'Anywhere, let's go.'

'And Barry, and Mark?'

'They made their way here easy enough, am sure they'll find their way back.'

'What if they don't?'

'They'll find a sofa, you know what Barry's like, they'll be grand. I want to be where you are.'

'It's that simple?'

'Please.'

'You don't want to go back out there?'

'Yes. No.'

o

After getting let out the front way, where Rachel buys a selection of miniatures from behind the bar and puts them into Órla's bag, they start making their way home across the beach. Rachel takes the small bottles of spirits out one at a time, slipping them between their mouths, taking a swig each; blowing hot alcohol breath onto their hands, their ears, their necks, their mouths, stooping to kiss at the end of each taste, hands in hair, hands in pants; their hands in and out of everywhere, touching, pressing, kneading, feeling for some recourse, and stooping and stopping now and again to drink and kiss, and pushing and straining and stooping and stopping to hold each other up.

o

Rachel takes the double duvet off the single bed and spreads it on the floor, places pillows on top, and scatters throws and blankets. Órla takes off Rachel's tights and shirt she's been wearing and burrows underneath, lies there fiddling with the hoop earrings trying to undo them without lifting her head. Rachel slides in next to her.

'I'm too cold.'

Órla hooks the earrings together and passes them behind her onto the dresser.

'You're coming down.'

'I think I'm just cold.'

'Okay.'

Órla nests Rachel into her and pulls another blanket over them. Kisses the parting of her hair. Rachel:

'Why are you with him?'

[inaudible]

'Why?'

'I don't not like him.'

'You don't adore him.'

'I've never got that whole girls fawning over their boyfriend thing.'

'He's no match for you.'

[quiet]

'I know.'

[pause]

'So why then?'

'I mostly like having sex with him.'

'Mostly…'

Rachel laughs into Órla's chest.

[silence]

'I'll tell you this okay… it's the longest time I'm not judging him…'

'Explain.'

[quiet]

'Why did he say that? Why did he stand there in that way? Why did he wear those clothes together? Why did he make that unattractive face? Why does he talk down to people? Why does he take up so much space? Why doesn't he take better care of his skin? Why is he so often so near, clingy? Why is he so mean sometimes?'

'Some list.'

Órla rubs both her hands up and down her face:

'Because I'm not a good person?'

'You are my very best person.' Rachel smiles.

'I don't not like having sex with him, I feel I should make that clear.'

'Clear as mud.'

'I mostly like it, or I like most of it, I dunno.'

'Which bits don't you like?'

'Right, he, he never asks can he come in my mouth. He just does it.'

'How unmannerly.'

'Hah… And you know when you move, expecting, indicating to the other person how they should move, he doesn't pick up on that.'

'Not everyone's really themselves in the moment, petal.'

'It's a kind of selfishness in bed a lot of fellas can have,' Órla moves closer to her. Rachel:

'Well you should know, you've done a thorough survey.'

'Feck off.'

'You have though, like, you're well known; sometimes I think you're just trying them on for size.'

'Yeah, maybe, you have a point. Yeah.' Órla looks up at the ceiling.

'Are you going to break up?'

'I'll, sorry but, I'll have to talk to him about it.'

'Okay… and Órla, you don't have to do things in bed with men you don't like. Tell them when you don't like it.'

[quiet]

'How? Oh like you know those hundred times you came in my mouth, well I'd prefer you'd asked me first, yeah I only told you this now to make you feel tiny and like you're a horrible person. Will we go the pictures tonight?' Órla claps her hands together.

'Very droll. I imagine, with my extremely limited experience of men, you'd have to start as you mean to go on.'

'Yeah.'

'Yeah.'

Órla: 'You didn't like it then? The penis sex?'

'I always missed the breasts, and penises are manky ugly.'

Órla laughs: 'They really are.'

'Erect they're so angry looking, and dumb.'

'They are really dumb. Simplistic.'

'I've never got wet thinking of a penis.'

Órla laughs again. Thinks on it, then says: 'I have seen some remarkable ones. I'd go them again.'

'Okay.'

[quiet]

'Rachel, do you still be with girls in Maynooth?'

'It's harder cos I'm staff now. But yes, I do.'

'Jesus, you're not getting off with young ones, are you?'

'Ugh no. Women.'

'Are their fannies gorgeous and intelligent?'

'All fannies are smart gorgeous.'

'All?'

'All.'

'Is mine the fairest in the land?'

'Yours is just my favourite.'

'That's nicer than it sounds.'

'I meant it to be nice.'

'It is.'

[quiet]

'Órla, petal, I'm pretty much done with here.'

[inaudible]

'I've applied for some jobs, away.'

[silence]

'We could emigrate. Live together in Camden. Be a cliché.'

'I don't know yet what I want, Rachel.'

[quiet]

'I know.'

'You don't hate me?'

'Never. I could never hate you. Not for very long.'

'That's nicer than it sounds.'

'I meant it to be nice.'

'I could never really be me without you.'

'I know, petal. Me too.'

'Me too.'

'Me too.'

'I love you.'

'Me too. Let's sleep now.'

'Sleep sounds nice.'

Soon enough they sleep.

o

'Your dad's car's not here.'

'He's probably gone to nine o'clock Mass—if he wakes up early on a Sunday he goes again.'

'Jesus.'

'—is right.'

'Ba boom cha. I made us tea and toast.'

'I'm fucking starving.'

'Coke'll do that to you.'

'Enough. I'm not apologising.'

'Ah, I didn't mean it like that. I'll have to head home soon, poke my head in, with the cousin seeing me out there'll be ructions if I don't.'

'Be added to the parish bulletin this morning.'

'Yeah, that Ryan young one is a dirty stop-out.'

'Who isn't in this town.'

'You're really over it then? Here?'

'I just can't, like, keep working part-time cutting and pasting and answering the phone. I just can't.'

'What'll you do in London?'

'Anything but this.'

'That is such an Irish sentiment.'

'We all have our moments.'

'When might you go?'

Rachel screams into her pillow. Órla lets her scream, waits for her to finish, rolls her onto her back and slides down her, pushes up her T-shirt and starts taking off her knickers.

'Órla.'

'Do you want me to stop?'

'Never, Órla, I never want you to stop.'

Órla kisses Rachel along her hairline, the crease of her thigh, bites at the soft flesh, runs her fingers inside, teasing, tucks herself down further and exposes Rachel completely, looks at the pure exquisiteness of her, studies her folds, touches her skin, closes her eyes and breathes her in deep, opens her out with her tongue, eats her with her whole wet mouth, eats her and eats her and eats her, she macerates her, and she tastes so very, very good and right and beautiful. Their sex is beautiful.

○

Órla stands on top of the stone wall on the coast road, heading home. The salt spray sands her face, granules rub at her skin. She can see an outline of another inlet quite a ways away. It's all part of this one long undulating curve that follows the flow of the island. Dribbles of blood sloping out to sea. Órla rocks back and forth. Willing the blood. Rocks back and forth. Hoping for the blood. Rocks back and forth. Waiting on the blood. Rocks back and forth. Tilting her uterus. Battened. Rocks back and forth. All those almost men who've come inside her. Rocks back and forth, thinking: 'You're going to break your high-heeled shoes.' Rocks back and forth. 'You're going to break your high-heeled shoes.' Rocks back and forth. 'You're going to break your high-heeled shoes.' Rocks back and forth. 'You're going to break your high-heeled shoes.' Rocks back and forth. 'You're going to break your high-heeled shoes.' Rocks back and forth. 'You're going to break your high-heeled shoes.' Like a country music song jammed on repeat.

Formalism...

...clink.

The First Person Possessive

or Proper Nouns Are Lost to the Yesterdays We All Dreamt of Anyway

I'd noticed you were off the scene, so I asked her out, last week, for lunch. She said she couldn't meet up for lunch, but later on, for a drink, I met her, she was coming from one thing, heading to another. I met her and she seemed happy to see me, we talked, we had a few drinks, she asked would I mind if she ordered some food, did I want some, I said yes. Yes. I wanted to eat.

We had food and she told me of the exhibition she'd just been to, she has lots of art friends who exhibit. She liked the photographs, she thought it was beautiful, clever, very well hung. I laughed at that, she laughed too. We shared a smile. She was glad she liked the exhibition, she'd had good things to tell her friend, and isn't it awkward when you think about someone—you like as a person—that their art is, well, shit? I laughed and asked her, is she always this diplomatic? She pulled a who-me face and said, meh, strong opinions are good, don't you think? She talks a lot, but she asks a lot of questions. She pays attention to everything I say. She's genuine. Her lack of bullshit is refreshing. It was noisy then, we couldn't hear each other talk. I asked her would we pop next door for another drink, she said, yeah go on so—

We were there, next door, a few more drinks in, and I said to her, oh shit, what about meeting your friends, had I kept her too late? And she told me, I texted them earlier when I was outside smoking that I was busy here and I might not see them tonight. She couldn't have said it plainer. Good. I asked her, so I'm what you want, you want to stay out with me tonight? She made a face like, don't double-dare me. And said, I've no better offers, do you? I snorted with laughter. She's hilarious. And straight to the fucking point. I should have asked her out ages ago, she seemed keen then, at first, when she met me; but you were there too back then, always there too, you. And she said, drink? then. My turn, I'll get us another drink.

o

Now, we walk into the thing late. Very late. We are very late. Too late? We walk in together. She is holding my hand. She is holding my hand. I breathe in deep. People see us. They nod. A few do a double-take. She is holding my hand. She squeezes my hand and offers to go to the bar. I squeeze hers back and say, I'll go. She smiles. Her smile. That smile. She looks at me like, go on go. That smile she smiles at me. That teasing smile. I don't want to let her hand go. She laughs and says, I'll still be here when you get back. She knows me. How can she know me, already? She parts from me.

o

I wait at the bar. It's late, very late. We were late getting here together. We've been together all day, since last night. I wouldn't let her go home. She didn't want to. So we were late, late going to hers for her to change for this thing, then we were hungry, we went to get food, and we were drinking, bottles of red wine, in the restaurant, and it was just us there together, eating with all the other people, and now it's us here at this thing so late, so very late, and people we both know will have seen us together, and I am happy. She looked happy. She told me she is happy. All week we've been together. All week. This first week. But tonight, tonight we walked into the thing together.

o

I order our drinks at the bar. I look for her, I see you watching her.

o

You. You. I forgot about you. All week I forgot about you. You. You were always watching her. Always watching her before when I was watching her. But we walked in together. Did you see? I hope you saw. I hope you saw her come in here with me. She hasn't noticed you. And now, now, you're not watching her anymore. I stop watching you. Now, it doesn't seem so late. Everyone's still here. There's time to go. I breathe out.

We have the rest of the night. We have all night.

All night for you, for you to see she's with me now. She is laughing with her friends. I can see her laughing. She has the deepest, dirtiest laugh. Have you heard her laugh, that laugh? I bet you haven't. Have you? You. Fuck. I'm fucked off. You. I forgot about you.

I see her say hello to you. You go to kiss her cheek. She turns to her friend. She avoids your kiss. You. Why are you here? Always here, when I am here trying to talk to her. You. And, you're talking to her. But she came in with me, we walked in together. Did you see? She looks over at me, motions that she's going outside, she walks out with her friends to smoke, and you, you walk out with them, and while you are walking you place your hand in the centre of her back, so softly, behind her, and she, she steps one quickstep forward, out of your touch. She walked in with me, she held my hand, people saw us; you, you are not important.

o

My friends call me over to the table with the sofa and the chairs. I take our drinks over to them, I want to hear, I want to hear what they have to say about us walking in together. There is an armchair free and I sit on it. My friend says, we saw you, is it true? You walked in together? We did, I say. We are together. My friends say, they are together, together. We never thought we'd see you two finally getting it together. But, you have, you are, this is great news. I smile, I nod. And I talk with them, they catch me up, they are telling stories, people are laughing, I'm laughing, and I am happy here waiting for her to come back to me.

o

You are back inside again. You are talking to someone I don't know, you look over at me. I pretend I haven't seen you. I will just ignore you.

She. She comes in from smoking and looks for me. She sees me here in the armchair, she comes over to me. She goes to sit down next to me. But I pull her down onto my lap. Because I've seen you watching her again. She laughs, she laughs and whispers into my ear. Her breath smells of tobacco. Her smoky breath is hot against my ear. She tells me she's tipsy. I tell her she was tipsy hours ago. She pinches my arm and laughs. You are still looking over. Did you see? Did you see her pinching me like that? Will that not make you stop looking over? I want you to stop. Fucking stop. She asks me, was she outside too long? Not at all, I say. I turn my head to kiss her. I want you to see me kiss her, I want you to see her kiss me. She kisses me a little. Then stops. She looks at me like she's sorry she had to stop because we are not alone. She stays, she stays sitting on my lap. I lean forward and pass her a drink. She says she really shouldn't, she's already had more than enough. I say, you can sip it slowly through the straw. She says, that's some stamina you've got. And laughs, her deep and dirty laugh. I put my hand on her face and smile at her. She's incredible. She's sitting here, in front of everyone, on my lap. And you're still fucking looking over. I wish you would just fuck off. I look around to see that everyone has seen us. I think now almost everyone knows. People she knows are smiling over. I know them to see, but I don't know them. Some other people I know have seen us. They nod. One winks at me. They know. Everyone knows, she's with me. Could you just look the fuck around you and view what's going on in the room? I don't know you. She knows you. I don't want to. I don't want her to. You, you, you, fucking you.

o

You are watching us sitting on the armchair, I won't let her up off my lap. She likes it here. She's made no move to leave. She likes sitting right here on my lap. Her friend has gone to the bar to get us all one last one. She said, please no, please no. Her friend said, sort yourself out, don't become a lightweight on me, they're having another one; I said, I am, the very last one, then we're going to head. Her friend is at the bar. She leans against my shoulder. She whispers to me, thank you for that. I put my hand on her knee and squeeze, and she nestles her head down on my shoulder. She's talking into my ear, that she's sleepy, and when can we go to sleep? I say to her, she can sleep at mine, she says, that's great, that's the very place I wanted to sleep. Your place.

I squeeze her knee.

She's telling me some story she heard outside, I see you looking over here at her. Can you see her? Can you see her half-lying here on top of me? You do see her, and you sit down opposite on a stool. You're pretending to talk to a friend. But you're glancing indiscreetly over at me. I see you and I have to struggle to pay enough attention to what she's saying so I can get the names right later if she asks me. Because I have to pay attention to you now. I don't want to pay attention to you. I want to pay attention to her. But I have to. Because you've sat down opposite us for a reason.

○

I often saw you looking at her, before, all year, when I was looking at her too, and she looked at you a lot last year, I saw you both looking and talking late into the night, your friends would leave you two to it, and I think I saw you once, twice, touching her face, her leg, her back, and I think she let you, she leaned into it, but I couldn't see, I couldn't see properly, and I was talking with friends, listening, watching you, watching you always talking to her—until late—and I think I remember one night I saw you leave with her; no, you'd often leave with her, but I never saw you walk in together, I never saw you holding her hand, so I thought, there mustn't be much to it, and now you can see she's happy sitting here publicly on me. I pulled her down here for you to see. For you to see her here sitting on me.

○

Her friend drops back the drinks and scoots outside for a smoke. No, she absolutely is not going with her friend. She says she's staying here with me. Did you hear her? Did you hear her say she's staying here with me? You keep looking over and I'm sick of you. I'm trying to enjoy the feeling of her here on top of me.

She's telling me about a show she's just heard about, and she knows the artist, and am I free? Would I like to go? She's making future plans with me. With me. I do not know how well she knows you. I do not really want to know. But why, why would you have put your hand on her back so easily?

And she stepped out of it, like it was well-practised, on her part; like that was the place your hand used to be, and she was tired of you putting it there so easily after she didn't want it there anymore, and the familiarity is too clear to me. I want you to see my hand on her now. I want you to see my hand where yours cannot, is not, will not get to be.

I move my hand from her knee and rest it on her leg. I rest it on the outside of her leg in your full view.

And I look right at you, for one long second, then stop.

But I know you're still fucking watching. I dared you to watch. I move my hand along her leg, so her dress moves up while I'm moving my hand, but I won't stop because I, I want you to see how high she's letting my hand go, I really fucking want you to see my hand going up her leg with the skirt of her dress. And she pulls the skirt down over my hand—because we are in public—but doesn't move it away and she leans in and kisses me, and I leave my hand there, up under her skirt, and she's kissing me and you can see, everyone can see. Because I want you to see where the line is. I want everyone in here to see—these markings my hands make on her body. I am drawing these lines on her body for you to see the places I have already been. I want you to imagine the rest. I want you to see what I can see when I see you watching us. I want you to feel it too. You are thinking my hand has been up further than under, just here, under her skirt. My hand has been up in her further, further than I hope yours has ever been. My hand has been inside her knickers, last night, the night before that too, all afternoon, and tonight, it's going up there again tonight. She likes it high up there in her. She didn't once ask me to stop. She took me up there inside her, and it was a place I knew with ease where to be. She moved with me—in her—and it's our place, now. Our place.

o

Her friend arrives back and we are still kissing, she hits us both, sharp taps on the backs of our heads. Get a fucking room, you two, for fuck's sake. We pull apart.

Now that you know I've touched her up further, I'm happy to leave it at that. I look over, you're moving away, I can't stop myself. I place my hand around her, my thumb visibly resting on the side of her breast. I look over at you again. I look right at you; and give you my best fuck-off-with-yourself look. Her friend is talking about going on around the way for another last one. She looks at me with despair. Her friend's off again, getting our coats. She says, we'll have to go there just for one more, then we really can fuck off. I say, yeah, sounds like a plan. She tells me she'll meet me at the door in a bit.

o

I look at my watch and it's late, very late, beyond fucking late, too late? It's tomorrow now. I make my way over to the exit, you're standing there talking to her, you're helping her on with her coat. You watch me walking towards you, you place your hand there—on her—on her back again—

Phonology

what i am to her is not spoken, whispered maybe, as an aside under the breath, between the lips low muttering of the mouth, the body our bodies. making new sounds. *she tells me i am special, important. another woman says you know i love you, anything that makes you happy, makes me happy. too.* what i am to her is not spoken, we meet in clandestine spaces, places. apart. what i am to her is a new thing. and we have time. what i am to her is not spoken, it is. / / Words stay unformed, the guttural noise, plosive, fricative breaths. The throat, arc of the tongue, roof of the mouth, line of the teeth, meeting of the lips. The pressure on the diaphragm. What I am to her is not spoken. What she is to me. Matters.

Yet.

Interlude
Belles-Lettres

Light effect—pattern of fish swimming in a shoal, rippling across stage and the face of an actor. Light is changing between blue, green, yellow and white. Actor is standing enthralled, captivated by light show. Animatedly follows fish with eyes and head, as if in dreamlike state. Musician starts playing a double bass. Continues. Actor steps to the side. Bassist and double bass are behind actor standing side-on. Slowly turn on spot while playing to face front. Actor takes double bass from musician. Musician continues humming the piece. Actor turns double bass sideways and starts to ride it like it is a horse and actor is a jockey. Scene continues. Light show continues. Humming continues.

A woman stands naked in the centre of a stage.
A spotlight shines on her.
This is offensive.

A woman stands naked in the centre of a room a light shines on her this is inoffensive.

A woman stands half-naked in the centre of a stage.
A spotlight shines on her.
This is offensive to some, inoffensive to others.

A woman is playing a double bass.
She is riding it.
She is doing both things at the same time.
This sounds like hay fever underwater.

A woman stands in the centre of a stage.
A spotlight shines up and down her.
Wherever the light is not shining this woman is naked.
We do not know that it is offensive.

A woman stands naked in the centre of a stage.
There is a spotlight shining on her.
The woman mouths that she is drinking fishes.
This is confusing.
Another woman walks onstage.
She is fully clothed.
She kisses the first woman.
Both women look to centre stage.
They look happy.
Someone out of the spotlight sees their happy look.
They don't like it.
They call to the audience: 'Let not these women be happy.'
The women look to each other.
The women look at themselves.
They interrogate their feelings.
Ultimately, they feel sad.
That is what we are always told happens when women think too much.
They have complicated thoughts.
These thoughts drain them of energy.
They feel tired.

Everyone knows that endorphins make you happy.
You don't have endorphins when you are sleepy.
Melatonin makes you sleepy.

Tired also rhymes with tied. Not really. But we like the
sound of tongue twisters. And manoeuvring our mouths.

The women would like to touch each other. This is not
allowed. They might get overexcited.

If they get overexcited, they might find enjoyment.
That would be another route to happiness. That is
nobody's good idea. It is better to stay in a touch-free,
hands-free zone.

Things are bad.

This could be shitloads worse.

Otiose means serving no useful purpose.

The women would like to mount the cello, they call it a
cello because they cannot tell it is a double bass, they are not
preoccupied with size.

The fish are swimming onstage in a body of water. A
body of water has become a moveable feast. Streams
stretching, a delectable dish, which part will I eat, the toes
point, the foot arcs the calf is shapely and sound, the
thighs _____, churn, the crotch yearns, the buttocks
plump, the whole way round, the concave(, its convex),

the breast still shaped and full, the arms strong, the hands deft, the collarbone nesting -------, the neck twists, the skull held, The solid, non-solid state, The movements neat, The sense _____,

This body
a fish
can swim
out of water
an old wretched thing

Inutile is an affectionate name for a fish made up of trickeries of light.

Offstage. A man is speaking. His voice does not carry, for he has a weak voice.

Fish gestate in ponds and babies' bodies are 80% water. You could be a puddle if you tried harder to wring yourself dry.

Offstage. A man is speaking. He sounds like white noise interference.

Indifference is an intellectual game no one interacting with ever gets quite right.

Onstage. The two women are looking to one another, they are drawn to think of touch.

Hand shadows show these actions on the backdrop curtain, multicoloured fishes continue to float by.

Woman One searches for Woman Two's fingers with hers. Woman One presses the fingertips of her right hand to Woman Two's, then nail bed to nail bed, they repeat this action as though they have so so so so often done so before.

Woman Two exhales: *this looks like a hand explosion. Make a fist with your preferred hand. It needs to be your preferred hand, for strength. Your preferred hand should always be stronger than your less preferred hand. That other hand should be prettier having spent more time in your pocket. Run your thumb down the outside of your fingers on your preferred hand until it comes to the nail tips. Push your four fingers open brightly—like the unveiling of a secret.*

Woman Two runs her thumb along Woman One's index finger. Woman One catches her hand in hers and intertwines their fingers, resting them, grasped together, on her lap. *Her lap is an imaginary place off the bottom of the curtain, we can only see one hand shadow being directed below by another hand shadow. We do not see what happens below the curtain.*

Woman Two looks to Woman One, comically failing to raise a singular eyebrow and producing a mistimed squint. Woman One smirks, and Woman Two rolls her eyes. *This is achieved by two index finger shadows forming themselves into bent shapes, bend at proximal interphalangeal (PIP), bend at distal interphalangeal (DIP), do not bend at metacarpophalangeal (MCP), i.e. do not bend at knuckles. Try to straighten one index finger at the DIP. Fail. Move the other index finger up and down quickly at the same joint. Straighten first finger and roll around in a circular motion. Do not wave the first index finger as though chastising. That is not the point.*

Woman One retorts, turning her body fully towards Woman Two, then leaning her head back as if against a headrest. *Now each whole hand is a whole body. Now each whole hand is a whole head. For speech press fingertips to thumb tip and release. For bodies, curate your hands by curving your fingers slightly, this will make leaning backwards or forwards easier if the hands are already slightly bent.*

Woman Two asks a question, studying Woman One's countenance. *When people are chatting you can move the hand shadows like how heads might tilt, wobble and bob in conversation.*

Woman One tuts, clicking her tongue against her dental ridge. *This is a sound effect. Speak to the Sound Designer. You want it to sound annoyed like a lover, but not harsh like an ex-lover, or dull like a spouse.*

Woman Two says several things, searching Woman One's eyes with her own. Woman One replies, holding her gaze. Woman Two counters; looking hard, sharp. *The handheadbob would be inopportune at this time, this is a serious conversation, to indicate the seriousness the fish should swim slower across the backdrop screen which should change from multicoloured to black* and white. Because this is a serious conversation no one is really very definite in what they are saying, but the tone is being set, instinctively colour should drain in a non-vertical line with a negative slope for depicting mood. The humming should become a series of dots.

Woman One squeezes Woman Two's hand, pressing her fingers into the fleshy indents between the knuckles. *Love has returned and so too should the yellow gel in the lighting rig. There are little but self-explanatory movements here. They should be very very slow movements, time should be taken to capture the moments when joy gets let in.*

The women return to face centre stage, the next bit is shown as full body shadows on the curtain. It will be hard for the audience to disengage their attention from the one naked woman and the second dressed woman onstage. To make this more difficult for them there should be graphic cinematic close-ups superimposed in flashes across two side screens:

> *Woman One reaches and tucks Woman Two's hair behind her ear, pressing the lobe between her index finger and thumb, the way one might do to a sick child.*
>
> *Woman Two chuckles, then winces and hangs her head.*
>
> *Woman One runs her hand over Woman Two's hair and brings it to rest at the nape of her neck.*
>
> *Woman Two's shoulders begin to shake, she slaps and snaps at the air, crosses her arms in front of herself, then rests her forehead on top.*
>
> *Woman One begins to knead the exposed vertebrae along Woman Two's neck.*

Woman Two snorts.

Woman One presses the palms of both her hands firmly on top of Woman Two's shoulder blades and says,
'_____.'

Woman Two turns to face Woman One and mouths, 'Kiss me.'

Woman One looks and asks, 'What?'

'Kiss me,' *Woman Two mouths again.*

Woman One takes firm hold of Woman Two's lapels and yanks her close.

All vertical surfaces that can be purposed as screens should flash between full body shadows and graphic filmic close-ups.

Breathing is short and hurried
Buttons and clasps undone
Hands stroking
Lips parting
Tongues sliding
Woman One bends forward takes each of Woman Two's breasts to her mouth in turn
kissing the circumference of the areolae
grazing nipples with her teeth
flicking them when erect with the tip of her tongue
Woman Two shifts her weight forward
knees resting
on either side of a plinth
She reaches up under her skirt and rolls her pants down
Woman One slides her hand up along Woman Two's shin
—tickling the crease behind her knee—

softly scratching her clipped fingernails along the
tenderness of inner thigh
   tips tipping hairs
   finding the smooth bald V
   spreading labia apart
   edging clitoris
   round and round and round
   waiting for the push
   Woman Two tilts her head to the right
   her body follows
   what develops is a meandering motion
   led by her head dancing, and
   culminating
   in the whirlpool curling of her hips

The women start speaking in whispers, it echoes from the back of the auditorium.

W1:

W2:

W1: 'Woman Two?'

Woman One asks from their embrace.

W2: 'Mmmmn.'

Woman One lifts her head from Woman Two's breasts then whispers tentatively into her ear.

W1: 'Have one.'

The fish start to swim in circles.

W2: 'You don't want one. Don't say something like that in a moment just because we're here and you can.'

W1: 'I do too want one. And, I so very much want you to have one.'

The fish start to swim in loop-de-loops.

W2: 'But Woman One, it won't be ours.'

Woman Two's voice raises curtly, she begins drumming her nails.

Undeterred, Woman One continues.

W1: 'It would be ours enough. Have one.'

The fish start to swim in opposite directions.

W2: 'I… want… our… own… thing,'

Woman Two admits.

W1: 'They would be. Go on. Have one.'

The fish start to swim in figures of eight.

Woman One leans forward and kisses the moisture gathering at Woman Two's temple.

Woman Two pleads.

W2: 'How?'

W1: 'Just have one.'

The fish start to swim like synchronised swimmers in a kaleidoscopic image. This is stunning. Sit in place and watch this for some time.

W2: 'But how, Woman One? I don't know how.'

Woman Two gets to speak aloud alone. The second woman is often silenced. The second woman usually has only a supporting role, a bit part. That doesn't happen here. We always want to know what the second woman is thinking. She is not only there to be adored. The second woman gets a monologue, because the second woman is very clever and thinks she thinks smart things often, we want and don't want to hear her speak:

'I have a preference for less dense materials, where my interests lie in structures that can be separated into their tiniest parts. Wherein one thing could be divisible into a multitude of things, making the original thing no one thing at all. Its existence entirely dependent on its composite parts. Belying the nature of a thing as an individual thing. Like mothers, who are strange creatures biologically. Not one being post-natal. Unlike fathers, mothers do not give of themselves once; they continue becoming during the nurturing stages of parenthood. Ever evolving. Three different beings. First, a girl. Next, a woman. Then, a mother. A giwomo — as I like to call them. Is it the same for fathers? First, a boy. Next, a man. Then, a father. A bomafa? Giwomos aren't spent at fruition, bomafas are spent at conception. It is not actually in the womb that a woman's becoming is conceived. Giwomos are complicated creatures. All women, even those who have no craving for nor affiliation with children, are observable vessels; regardless of genitalia, organs, conditions, hiccups, botch-ups, choice, or luck. To the less scrutinising glance a woman is a body, a vase that gives the impression there is the possibility of becoming someone's mother. With possibility comes opportunity, whether taken, easily conceived.'

An underwater procession of naked women's bodies float up to and retreat from the curtain. Tryfailing to break through.

W1: 'The tide is washing up fast. This stage smells like heat and sex; or wet sand, like how sex can smell like hot wet sand.'

Offstage. A man is talking. He is important. We know he is important because other men have told us to think so, and thinking so is a reaction to being told how to think, and not thinking so is a tiresome struggle, when we can just as easily tune out his offstage voice and listen to the double-bassist humming string music while bows are scoring the scales off drab fishes tired from floating around and around in this underground rain drain.

Brainwashing as a consequence of impregnation prevails to some extent.

Offstage. A short man with a long body says words. We cannot hear him. We are not listening. He has an invidious nature.

'and. you. see. us. sea. and. you. see. seer-sees sea. but. what. you. should. see. sea.'

A fish is playing a fiddle with its fins. A clothed woman is playing a cello with her teeth. A naked woman is playing a double bass with her feet. There are shadows in the shoals the size of an orchestra's string section. I don't know what invertebrates means, but I do know how to spell it. This story has no ending it just

Diktat/Dictate I

/ dɪk.tæt /   / dɪkˈteɪt /

Joni Mitchell Nudes

she tells me not to worry about my blue period it will
pass or be remembered as a hat tip to art or forgotten on
a breeze / we're a whim of minerals crystalising against
the firm smooth stone / a central need in our desires our
escape out the monogamy this life will bring us further
into a future fire of deep skies opening in the garden and
earthly delights noticing the wet dark heap of us beneath
the shelter in a frame slowly lifting / me beyond your
taking / if we can travel through this mess you are
smiling or haven't smiled since you left and it is the tax I
pay for the realness of us in your body my pet my dear
my heat breaks and we love lusting over insides and you
touching my almost end here / we are free

Molly & Jack
At The Seaside

Molly and Jack are lovers. His friends call him Jimmy. They go down, to the beach, close by the harbour, on Tuesday evenings, and wriggle in the sand. Molly and Jack are close friends. His nickname is Jimmy. They play on the beach. They like to play in the sand. They like the seaside. Well, then again now, he wriggles really, against her; and she lies there thinking of apple trees. Jack acts the fool. Molly likes apple trees. It may sound a biteen fucking silly to you, but apples on trees are her favourite thing to think about. She is in love with green, yellow, red, and freckled apples. Do you like apple trees? Molly thinks about them all the time. Molly loves apples. Molly knows her colours.

Molly would love to be like those girls, the ones she watches with all her concentration, off of the telly. Molly watches naughty girls on television. Those vase-figured girls—with their too bright teeth—who go chomp in through the skin and suck out the juices of the succulent flesh. The girls on television have Extra® bright white teeth. The girls on television bite right into their apples. Flesh that is usually white, sometimes yellowy, and quite often brown. Apples are juicy.

Her dog is always knocking over the vegetable tray where she keeps her fruit tucked inside a brown paper bag. Molly has a dog. Molly's dog runs. Molly's dog plays in her kitchen. Molly's dog makes the apples fall. Molly says "bold boy, bold boy!". It keeps them fresh – if not unbruised. Molly's apples get banged.

She would love to have that kind of too bright personality, the one that has the ability to chomp teeth first into the flesh, the one that isn't quite so plain and dowdy and tubby. Molly is a nice girl. She should like to be nicer. Molly should not think about biting. No. No. She should not. No nice girl should. Nice girls do not bite. When you bite too much, they bite back.

It's just that when he lifts her skirt and pulls her knickers and draws her to him he's already inside before she's even felt the moisture or the warm hot breath and the sweet soft nothings she would expect for giving him what she's giving him. Jack lifts Molly's skirt. Jack takes Molly's knickers off. That is a bold thing. Molly should not let him. Molly should keep her knickers on. That is what a good girl would do. Molly is dry. Molly lets Jack take her knickers off. Molly is not ready. Molly is very naughty. She is a bold girl. Molly likes Jack and dirty bold things. She does not love him. It isn't like she's handing it to him on a lace-topped platter. Molly is a good friend to Jack. She likes to share. Molly shares herself. Molly is easy. It is easy to be naughty. Molly is a naughty girl with boys. Molly will say she only knows two boys. Two boys are a lot of boys to know. How many boys do you know? Good girls only know one boy. Remember that.

She's been seeing Jack for over seven months now. She does worry about her sons. They have been left before. So, isn't it better for her to have her own little bit of adult privacy once a week than to be discommoding them for the sake of her wants. As she duly considers whether she does want this, she considers what it is she wants or needs for herself. Molly thinks about herself with other people. Molly thinks about herself with other grown-ups. Grown-ups have special private times together. They are called kin-ky times. A kink is a twist like on a twisty drink straw. Twisty drink straws are a fun way to drink minerals. Kinky times are a fun way for grown-ups to play in private. They can play all kinds of secret kinky games. Molly always does what she is told when she plays kinky secret games. Molly plays by the rules. She is con-sid-er-ate. Considerate is nearly the same as kind. A good girl is kind and well-behaved.

She needs those limbs. Molly wants Jack's arms and legs.

It's not moist though, not an easy slide; but a slim fit. It is dry. "It's hard." Put it in its place. Is it in the right place? Is it in the wrong place? Do you keep pushing something in when it does not fit? If you keep pushing will you break it? When you break something can you fix it? Should you think before you act? Is there always time to?

Be they the limbs of a tree or the limbs of Jimmy ... "JIM-MY!" "Ouch." JIM ... AAAHh ... EEEEE!!! Molly likes branches. Apples grow on branches. Molly likes trees. Fruit trees are her favourite. Molly says she likes Jack's arms and legs. Molly calls Jack's name. Does she? Does she shout his name out?

Molly's forty-eight and not a penny from the ex to keep her three boys going. Molly is very old. Molly is ancient. Molly has some money. She would like to have more money. Molly has an old friend who owes her money. He keeps his money tree for himself. Molly thinks he should share.

Sharing is good. Girls should share. Sharing is how you become a good girl. Sharing is how a good girl shows her manners. Do you share? If you share do you like it?

Most of all she'd love to go chomp—chomp, chomp, chomp—into the flesh; bite right into the skin, through to the soft fleshy inside, feel it, let herself go in the motion, let herself go in the rocking wriggling movement. In and out, in and out, in and out, in and out, in and out, in and out – though it's never quite in. She wants to feel it. Really feel it. Molly wants to bite. Bite. Bite. Bite. Molly would love that. Molly wants to move. She would love that a whole lot. Molly wants to move like "it's playtime". Things move in and out. It is not always easy to get things in. Molly wants ex-per-i-en-ces. Experiences are new feelings you make or do. Molly wants to be sin-cere. Sincere is almost like what honest means. No sin. No, no. No full lies. Molly would love the exploration. She'd love to be idly touching him with her fingers, stroking him, licking him. Molly wants to touch Jack (slowly). Molly wants to pat Jack. Molly wants to lick Jack. "Licking tastes nice." "Juicy apples." "Juicy fruits." Molly wants to eat the apples. Even though she knows it is naughty. Bold girl. "Bold boy! Bold boy!" "Bold girl." "BAD DOG!" Molly wants to lick Jack. Is Jack a dog? She doubts she's the type of girl who'd go chomp; so she doesn't. Molly does not touch Jack (slowly). Molly does not pat Jack. Molly does not lick Jack. "Licking tastes nice." Is Jack the dog?

Things haven't improved much from Molly's teenage years, stretched out flat on her back on the beach. Molly is old now. Molly was young before. Molly does the exact same things now as then. Does Molly do them? Does Molly do these naughty things ...? Wanting to succumb, wanting to fuck it all to hell. But Molly worries, keeps thinking she'll be "caught". She lies /≠/ She wants to give in. Does she? She wants to go crazy. Is she? Is trouble scaring Molly ...?

Someone will hear him grunting. Jack makes pig noises. "Oink. Oink. Grunt. Grunt." Can you do that? "Oink. Oink. Grunt. Grunt." Should you do that? Someone will see them leaving the pub. Molly is scared. A local could follow and watch them. "Licking tastes nice." An uncastrated male pig is called a boar. "Juicy apples, Moll; juicy apples." A boar is big and hairy. Molly is a good girl. "Juicy Fruit®." Molly wants to play with Jack. Molly will play nicely. Could be watching them right now. Molly wants to play with Jack. Alone. "Molly tastes nice." A big hairy pig. "Molly wants to play alone when no one else is watching." Does Molly? "Molly knows how to play that game as well. Very well." A big hairy fat pig. She can't relax. Molly is a good girl. Molly knows how to play both games. "Molly is the best girl." Molly can't see them with her eyes closed. "Take Molly." "Molly is a good girl." "Molly is the best girl." "Take Molly." She can't give herself to him. Molly is scared. Jack is not a dog. / Jack is a pig. / Jack is a pig in an orchard. A fat fat BOAR pig in the orchard full of apple trees. The boar will eat the apples. He'll eat the apples off the ground. He'll eat the fallen apples. He'll shake the tree. He'll eat the apples he knocked down. He knocked them down / he knocked them down / heknockedthemdowntoeatthem "Ouch / Ouch!" Brown paper all gone. "Yow! YoW!" He'll bruise the apples. There. Brown. There. Brown down. "There there." "Brown down there." "There there." Brown. "Put paper down there." Brown paper down down there. "There there." "Hush." "Shush." tHE big FATfat pig will eat all the apples. "Hush. Hush." A faTFat pig will munch his way right through them. Crunch. Crunch. "Shush. Hush." FaTFat piggy will devour the core. "All gone." FaTFat piggy will eat the bits that shouldn't be eaten. "Here." "There." "Here. Here." A faTFat piggy is called a boar. "Come here." A wild boar will keep eating the orchard's apples one on top of the other on top of the other on top of the other ontopofanother ontop of another ontopof the other on top of the other on top of another

other another other another another another other / other /
other / other / other / other / other / other / other other other
other   other   other   other   other   other
another … / Grunting as they go   : "All gone." / "All
gone." / "Full up." / "Belly full." / "Tum tum yum yum." / "JUICY
apple, Juicy APPLE, Juicy Fruit®: ALLGONE" / "Put your knickers
on." Playing in the dark is scary. It can scare you stiff. The
gasps she makes owe themselves to the sharp stinging
pains each time he jabs himself into her. Molly puffs. Jack
pokes Molly. Jack hurts Molly. Molly does not like it. It's the
secret she loves. Molly loves secrets. Molly keeps secrets.
Molly knows good girls keep quiet. You have to stay still to
play nicely.

Late on a Friday night watching Gay Byrne on the telly,
with a rug over her feet, thinking of her tryst to come she
stores the warmth – knowing that one night soon she'll be
freezing her tits off down the harbour. Molly stays up late on
Friday nights. Molly watches TV. Molly watches The Late Late
Show. Molly has a woolly blanket. Molly thinks about Jack. Molly
keeps warm inside. Molly gets cold outside.

"How do you keep warm?"

Molly's insides feel like outsides.

"What makes you hot?"

Molly always wears a skirt. Molly wears a skirt to the
beach. Molly likes skirts first. Trousers second.

Oh! It's a pure cold wind that laps at her seams, but she
thinks of the secret smiles it'll give her all week long, and
that's something. Isn't it? Isn't it. "Doesn't it? Doesn't it?" It
is windy. Molly thinks about smiling. Does she?

She wants a shoulder to rest on for those few moments
after. Molly wants to lean. She needs the comfort. Molly wants

to be mollycoddled. She craves it. She really really wants it. "Do you want?" Do you want it? "You want it." You want it? "Take it." "You want it."

Beach sex doesn't allow comfort. Playing on the beach can be awkward=tricky. "The devil to pay." There's always something jutting into her back and she's constantly tilting her head forward pretending to be huddling close when all that's really going on in her mind is: Please Jesus, don't let the sand get into my scalp. Molly's back hurts. Molly's always bruising. "Brown." Molly leans into Jack. The sand is messy. "Down there." The ends of your hair you can manage, but once it's in your scalp you're left with it for the rest of the week. Sand is hard to wash out of hair. "Brown in hair down there." "It's scratchy." Scratchy? "It's dirty." It's dirty? It's hurty. "Hush-hush-there-there-put-paper-down-brown-paper-down-down-down-there." What's worse than that? Sand up her bum? Pah! Sure, that's nothing. You can shower that out of you. Dirt gets all places, but you can wash it off. Can you? "Brown dirt gets all places, but you can wash it off. Can't you?" "Down there." "Brown down there." "Therethere." It stays there. Can you? Can you wash it off? "Put your knickers on."

She wishes she was the type of girl who'd go chomp. Molly wants to bite. Molly dreams of biting. Because then she'd take control of the johnny. Molly wants to play with rubber. She'd slowly tear the wrapper and slip it over his taut transparent skin, rolling it down, touching the vein as she'd go, she'd tease it on. And for the life of her she'd pay attention to what she was doing. She would play carefully. We must play carefully. "When we are careful we can play how we like." If only she'd reach over and take it out of his hand. That'd be something. Molly thinks it would be a game for a brave girl. On the nights when what's worst happens she couldn't give a shite that she's not moist, or a flying fuck about a shoulder respite as he pushes and pushes into her. The grains of sand rubbing against her insides. And how? How does he not feel it? "This makes you hot, Moll." God knows it's not an easy slide those times. Molly likes to play on the beach. Not every night. The sand hurts. It gets everywhere. Jack does not mind it. Jack does not mind her. Jack does not mind Molly. He does not mind her. They do not mind her. No one minds her. Molly doesn't like it. "The dirt inside her."

All of this bucking around on the beach amounts to nothing. She wants to feel the tension release from deep within her. She wants to breathe "O!" and mean it. Something is missing. Can you tell what it is? No, it is not apples. Try again. Molly wants excitement. Playing horses is all OK. It is not great. Molly wants to let go. Molly wants a surprise.

If only that eejit would travel deep within her. If only he would take her some other way. Make her another way. The thrusting never feels comfortable enough. She wants it hard and fast. She wants to want it. Molly wants Jack to go on holiday. Molly wants Jack to take her with him. Molly wants to relax. Molly wants many things. "Is Molly greedy?" "Moll has to stay still to play nicely."

There is a clammy residue gathering on her top lip and in the crevice below. Molly shifts about on the sofa, wishing the wetness away. She can do it to herself. She knows she shouldn't take such pleasure in her own body. The way she does it, it's not venial, it's a mortal sin. There is a part of her she can reach quickly and deftly. It floods her face red and her brain fuzzy. Molly has a mantra she says to herself at her most personal of times:

Fuck me rough/ Fuck me hard/ Fuck me with urgent disregard.

¶

Good girls are not greedy.

Remember that.

Winona the Wicked Wanton Woman

'It was wrought in a monk's slow manner
Of silver and sanguine shell,
Where the scenes are little and terrible,
Keyholes of Heaven and Hell.'

I

Once upon a time, in a Seaside Village, there lived many Manly Men. These Manly Men were big and strong. Tall and broad. High and mighty. Every day these Manly Men worked Manually. Feet on the ground, hands in the soil. They were passionate with their Land. They ploughed it, hoed it, raked it, sowed it. They took great care of their Earth, tended their crops from season to season, listened to the grasses grow long and breeze-blown in fallow years, watched colours changing within the texture of the days, the light from the sky, the foliage on the hedgerows, greens to greys to lemons, muted oranges then bright browns setting themselves against backdrops of milky blue skies brimful of keen wandering airs.

Every morning, for as long as memory knew, the Manly Men would rise at cock crow, weak sun-stream flirting through undressed windows, the moon still a dim dappled orb to the west of their Land, and open doors wide, plant bare feet on the Earth, stretch limbs up and out to welcome the coming of the day, grounding the Manly Men to the Earth and the Earth to the Men. Fastening them together in strength and union. While gaily in the Village on the rustle-tussle of the wind a ring of daisy cups might take to dancing next to the sweet suckle nectar promise of white clover flowers' teeth swaying this way and that beside brilliant bushes and pretty pebbles and invitations to pick a toy salad of soft wavy leaves from the hedgerows seasoned with baby fern fronds masquerading as parsley and grasses that looked like thyme.

One day in *Earrach*, or what is now known as Spring, when the clouds hung low in the fields and the flower buds of the plum trees were shuffling off their winter husks seeking out rebirth on rhubarb-hued branches, a new blackbird came to the Village. His beak a brighter orange than what is common, his coat a shinier oilier black. Even his hop was hoppier than most. For the purposes of this story we shall call him Blacky Blackbird. Blacky Blackbird flew to the most fertile Land at the east of the Village shortly before *Bealtaine*, the halfway marker to the changing of the season from Spring to the beginning of Summer. The little blackbird spotted some sunflower seeds peeking out from the Land in the fields. He set to work pecking at the seed of one unhulled kernel, then—quite systematically—at another and another and another, he eagerly made his way all the way up one row and right back down the next. He was—as has become apparent—a very greedy little blackbird. No matter how much Blacky ate he was never sated. This was quite arduous work, and considering his diminutive size he would become quite weak afterwards, stumble and mope about; then bellow four jaw-cracking yawns in short succession, roll onto his back causing quite a fuss altogether; after this he'd nestle down into the mulch, his tummy distended and bloated, feeling rather sorry for himself. But, following a rather short nap, he'd rouse himself and start to munch again on the next two rows. A gluttonous little thing like him can never learn and in not too long a time at all the rows of seeds in the soil were no more and Blacky had left the first field completely barren.

At the same time as Blacky, that greedy little blackbird, had shown up in the Village, a new Preacher also arrived. The Preacher was a tall lean bearded man who carried a wooden staff—this looks something like a stick you might see an infirm person walk with today for assistance in bearing weight when taking steps. The Preacher's staff was not a modest or plain implement to aid one's motion but a noise-maker announcing footsteps boisterously and causing tremors to reverberate across the Earth. The wooden staff was decorated with carved curlicues turning and twisting the smooth and sheen bark from its natural form, then narrowing and bending to display a ridge of scales burnt into the top end where, at the sharp crook, the Preacher's hand clutched a serpent's head. The Preacher made known his arrival by thumping the path along his way to the mound in the centre of the Village then dragging his staff deep into the Earth, marking it with a diagonal line, first one way; then right through its centre another. He stood at his trenched cross and began to sermonise daily at midday.

Out in the Fields, a flock of fellow blackbirds gathered and followed Blacky, devouring all the Manly Men's nascent crops before they could reach fruition. The Manly Men were appalled by these birds attacking their bounty. They knew not what to do. Eventually, the Manly Men were feeling very, very lost, dejected, almost at the edge of despair because they could no longer farm. Their way of life was slipping away.

The Preacher advised that Prayer was the answer, and his God would hear their prayers, and eventually save them. At first, the Manly Men were reluctant to stand still and listen to the Preacher's daily oratory on the mound at the Central Cross in the Village, because they so loved physical activity, being out in the elements appreciating nature, growth and replenishment throughout the seasons. But over time they were comforted by His words, the routine call to pause to listen to this Preacher telling them how they could overcome difficulties. And so, they looked again and again to the Central Cross in the Village for guidance.

But sadly, the Manly Men only saw more and more blackbirds arriving to wreak havoc on their crops. Each morning they would sow new seeds and then they would return after the midday sermon to find a host of birds covering their fields like a big black cloak. The Manly Men's vision began to fade in familiarity with the gloominess of the blackbirds' coats. The dark coats of the birds became a cloak of near-sightedness for the Manly Men to peer through. And, while peeping through this myopia they resolutely believed they would be rescued from this fog, fugue state, through inertia and prayer.

It was a stubborn rootedness, and the more they prayed for change, the more they believed change would be bestowed upon them; and the longer it wasn't, the more arduously they committed to prayer under the guidance of the Preacher, wholly convinced that this way would work. It became all-consuming until this cloak of Black and Whiteness eventually rose up like a giant tarpaulin shrouding the entire Village. Its morbidity spread outwards from the Central Cross in the Village. The Fields developed a resistance to growth until all frequencies of light were no longer visible to the local Manly Men. They only saw the Black end or the White end and nothing in-between.

Because of that the Manly Men were angered—but the cloak of Black and Whiteness was draped right over them, the land they had loved and tended was resisting them. The Manly Men did not know what to do. They looked again to the Preacher at the Central Cross in the Village, and in his staunch Black and Whiteness he told them the Earth belonged to them—it was their possession, from it they could reap their bounty. And, if it resisted, they were to use force to make it obey. A Mania was bestowed on them from their God above in Heaven. Eventually, the Mania reached fever pitch and the many Manly Men began tearing and pulling and wrecking and burning and building and stomping and banging and fastening and thrashing and knocking and lashing and bashing and belting and hurting and trouncing the Fields. Until finally, they had raped the Earth.

> 'He only heard the heathen men,
> Whose eyes are blue and blind,
> Singing what shameful things are done
> Between the sunlit sea and the sun
> When the land is left behind.'

II

Later upon a time, in a Seaside Village, there lived a Nymph: Winona. This Nymph was wet and willing. Slavish not supplicant. Low and minute. Every day this Nymph worked Manually. She took her passions from the corporal—washed bodies, dressed bodies, fed bodies, caressed bodies; her body was made to take good care of other bodies. One day—in early *Samhain*, or what is now known as Autumn, which had begun with morning chores just like every other day—while Winona was outside climbing then netting a mechanical fig tree, staring at the dark feathered materials above, the cloak of Black and Whiteness momentarily fell from the sky and encompassed everyone but her: in that instant she saw the dazzling brilliance of every colour-frequency of the

 rainbow and this exposure blinded one of her senses—her sense of sexual excess. Because of the celestial shift a precocious maturity was bestowed on her. This maturity was a sexual, Nymphal one. It spread outwards from her centre and coloured all her domestic deeds.

The Manly Men in the Village knew not what to do, they looked again to the Central Cross in the Village and sought guidance. The Preacher told them to reject Winona and her affliction. Because of this, in adulthood the Nymph became an outcast. She moved to live in a wooden hut on the edge of the Forest way way west at the far end of the Village.

III

Now upon a time, beyond in the Forest, there lives a Wicked Wanton Woman. A damp ditch borders Winona's wooden hut a balcony of coarse nettles and scraggedy tangleweed thickets surround an ivy wall with migraine-tasting dandelions the colour of margarine mocking thorny broken-limbed thistles, where a furious hewn massacre of brambles are strewn hither and thither. A hazard of hedges hunker next to a hoary hawk perched on a barbed-wire fence with a supercilious glint in his eye.

Her body is supple and slender, readied and hot.

She looks to her central core and therein lies the seed of a Mania. She had learned from the many Manly Men who came before her.

She knew what to do. From the Village she could take her bounty, it is hers, they were all her possessions and if they resisted she would use force to make them obey.

Eventually her Nymphomania reaches climax:

~~i like boys. their tiny cocks. their rocks. in their white jocks and cotton sports socks. i like girls. their slack backs and backsides. their slimy cracks. i like teenagers. their hair. not quite there. their buds. them in their underwear. i like young men. their scent. their collar and jawbones. hellbent. i like young women. their flair. hundred-yard stare. caught in my headlights. devil may care. i like gay men. cosseted. closeted. on all fours is good. i like sapphic women. at their beginning. panning for gold is good. golden showers. run amok. kissing and penetrative fucks. spread their legs. in the muck. i like married couples. together. apart. coming. is better when they're tethered from the start. i like married women they don't come alone even when they tend to roam. my lovers. married men. craving orifices. unknown. what they would not get at home. i like retirees, oaps, some auld men give good bone, the elderly women, want to do it on the phone. i like little runts. their cunts. the hairless shunt.~~

she devil nay care do it screw it fuckherheirs xx no xxx one xxx cares xxx say your prayers xxxx living nightmares xx

Until she is raping herself:

And   they   all   died   in   the   ever   after.

ABCB AABCCB//
Untitled Child's Song

A choir of 100 ten-year-old children are singing in a continuous round:

Do re mi do. do re mi do. mi fa sol. mi fa sol. sol la sol fa mi do. sol la sol fa mi do. Do sol do. do sol do. Do re mi do. do re mi do. mi fa sol. mi fa sol. sol la sol fa mi do. sol la sol fa mi do. Do sol do. do sol do. Do re mi do. do re mi do. mi fa sol. mi fa sol. sol la sol fa mi do. sol la sol fa mi do. Do sol do. do sol do. Frère Jacques, Frère Jacques, Dormez-vous? Dormez-vous? Sonnez les matines! Sonnez les matines! Ding, dang, dong. Ding, dang, dong.

Over which can be heard a four-year-old girl singing:

dang, dong. De re mi do. do re mi do. mi fa sol. mi fa sol. sol la sol fa mi do. sol la sol fa

LaLaLa is falling down Falling down falling down Lalala is falling down Her fair baby / ni

AAA B C D E C D E C D E l d C D E Do so C d d do E l d C D E mi d AAA BC D E F G H I sol.

Magdalene is broken down, Hold them down, choke them drown, Magdalene is broken down

LaLAlala *vous? Dormez-vous? Sonnez les matines! Sonnez les matines! Ding, dang, dong.*

LaLaLa is falling down Falling down falling down Lalala is falling down Her fair baby / a

AAA mi B C D E do s C D OE re n C D OE re n AAA BC D E mi F s G H I sol

Hush it up with guiltless tones, Weighty tomes, Weighty tomes, Hush it up with guiltless tones

LaLAlala *sol fa mi do. sol la sol fa mi do. Do sol do. do sol do. Frère Jacques, Frère*

LaLaLa is falling down Falling down falling down Lalala is falling down Her fair baby / J.

AAAg, doB, C iiD, dEng, do C J. D E mi c C D E mi AAA BC D E fa F G H I sol fa

Guilty crones will lock away Lock away Lock away Guilty crones will lock away *mi fa sol. mi fa*

AAA   B C D E   C D E   AAA   BC D E   F G H I

Hush it up with kicks and punches Slaps and punches Hush it up with hits and punches

LaLAlala

LaLaLa is falling down Falling down falling down Lalala is falling down Her fair baby /

AAA   B C D E   C D E   AAA   BC D E   F   G   H I

Kicks and punches will not stray Will not stray not stray Thumps and punches will not stray

LaLAlala

LaLaLa is falling down Falling down falling down Lalala is falling down Her fair baby /

AAA   B C D E   C D E   AAA   BC D E   F   G   H I

Hush it up with rods of steel Rods of steel Hush it up deny they feel

LaLAlala

LaLaLa is falling down Falling down falling down Lalala is falling down Her fair baby /

AAA   B C D E   C D E   AAA   BC D E   F   G   H I

Wills of steel won't bend or bow Bend or bow Wills of steel won't bend or bow

LaLAlala

LaLaLa is falling down Falling down falling down Lalala is falling down Her fair baby /

AAA   B C D E   C D E   AAA   BC D E   F   G   H I

Build us up with coffers of gold Coffers of gold Build us up with coffers of gold

LaLAlala

LaLaLa is falling down Falling down falling down Lalala is falling down Her fair baby /

AAA B C D E C D E C D E fa C D E fa C D Dol E AAA BC D E F G H I sol

Coffers of gold will be stolen away Stolen away Coffers of gold will be stolen
away

LaLAlala

LaLaLa is falling down Falling down falling down Lalala is falling down Her fair baby /

AAA B C D E C D E C D E AAA BC D E F G H I

Set a man to watch all night Watch all night watch all night Set a man to watch all night

LaLAlala

LaLaLa is falling down Falling down falling down Lalala is falling down Her fair baby /-

AAA? Do B C D E Somme C le D m Eines C D E les AAA BC D E F G H I

Suppose the man should fall asleep Fall asleep fall asleep Suppose the man should fall asleep?

LaLAlala

LaLaLa is falling down Falling down falling down Lalala is falling down Her fair baby /

AAA B C D E C D E C D E C D E AAA BC D E F G H I ues.

Give him a pipe to smoke all night Smoke all night smoke all night Give him a pipe to smoke
all night

LaLAlala

LaLaLa is falling down Falling down falling down Lalala is falling down Her fair baby /

AAA B C D E C D E C D E AAA BC D E F G H I rere

Who has stole my watch and chain Watch and chain and chain Who has stole my watch
and chain Her fair baby?

Off to prison you must go You must go You must go Off to prison you must go Her fair baby /

LaLAlala

LaLaLa is falling down Falling down falling down Lalala is falling down Her fair baby

AAA   B C D E   C D E   AAA   BC D E   F   G   H I

How shall we build it up again, with a gay lady, build it up with gravel and stone, dance all over her baby's bones, her fair baby

LaLAlala

Lalala is broken down Lalala lalala shall we build it up to bury them bury them build it up to bury them, fallen ladyees

AAA   B C D E   C D E   C D E   AAA   BC D E   F   G   H I

How shall we build it up again, with dead bones with dead bones, no one can see no one shall know of their, their dead babies

LaLAlala

Lalala is broken down, lalala, lalala, shall we build it up to bury them bury them build it up to bury them, fallen ladyees

AAA   B C D E   C D E   AAA   BC D E   F   G   H I

Put them in bins and punish them, punish them punish them, They are born of sin and sin is them sin is them sin is them, their sin babies

LaLAlala

Lalala is broken down, lalala, lalala, shall we build it up to bury them bury them build it up to bury them, fallen ladyees

AAA   B C D E   C D E   AAA   BC D E   F   G   H I

Bins are too good for them good for them, Dump them in pits and bury them their sin babies

Frère Jacques, Frère Jacques, Dormez-vous? Dormez-vous?

How, I?

You don't touch me anymore. And how I long to be touched. By you. It's been how many weeks since I felt the pressure of your lips on my lips? Beak on my beak. How many months since your mouth kissed my cunt— one, two, three? I can't remember how long it has been since. But I can't forget how good you tasted me, on the twill sofa, in the farmhouse, where the sparrows nest. All out, you went all out, that one time, it was so good for me. Good for you too. In the eaves chirping, and the mild scent of their downy sweet plumes. You relaxed into me, late afternoon sun peeking through slats in rafters, dust motes commingling with falling dander and limbs. When I came for the second time, you lifted your head, your hair from my hairs, and said: *I love doing this for you. I love when you come in my mouth. I love that you love it. You are pure sex.* The hum of the refrigerator, the pecking at seed, while we dipped and stooped, tasted and licked. We were languid: lolling, seated, lying. Obscene: erect and against and behind. Thrashing. Holding. Fluttering. And I was with you. That once, twice, three times. Those two, three, four hundred times. The go-slow beauty of it. I can't remember the last time. Can't want to. And you? Do you remember? Remember the almost naked explicitness of us. Hunched. Readied. On haunches. On the edge of something real, true. And you, you counted up to the forty-fifth time. I laughed so hard when you told me your calculations. Your keeping score. I should have known. I should have known how you would be, come the end. Arched. Hunkered down. Readied for our nest to fall from great heights. Smashed. Prostrate. Destroyed. Was it so disappointing that you didn't want it? Crave it. Did I stop doing it for you? Desperate, and clawing for food, shelter, air. Was I too little of a challenge? That's been said to me before, that they wanted to make me come. To make me. Hah. Make me. Did I need to hold back? Pleasure you more? But you, you liked the missionary position, and I must admit it's never been my favourite. Pleasure. I do not like the curtains closed, in the master bed, at a pre-appointed time. I do not like the lights off. Duvet on. No longer than one hour, no post coital rosy glow. I like the sweat. I like the hours. I like deep deep deep fucking. I like the whole day long in bed. I like hydration breaks, refuelling. Making food part of it. Us. Feeding me. I could live off the taste of your skin, sweat, saliva swilling in my mouth with beer, wine, and all those sour peppery mouthfuls of you. I like roll-over-in-the-middle-of-the-night sex. I like the surprise of your cock erect against me in my half-sleep, wet dream. I like the warm dark need-me breath. I like the slide in unexpectedly expected half-conscious sex—you rolling us, on top, behind, and coming in a soft violent way— then sleep again to dream of your cumming. I like all of that to be part of my week. I wait. I wait the whole working week for you. To come into my bed. Our bed. But you're elsewhere. Even when you're here you're there. It's like we're nowhere. You're there. I am nowhere. Here. Waiting for you. To come to me. In me. Incubation.

Waiting. I should have known. Waiting. I should have known, we would reach our use-by date—waiting. I should have known we had left our perishables on the counter too long. I should have known we would shrivel. I should have known we would rot, turn to mulch, our spilled fluids wasted, poured down the drain. A compost of birds' nests and eggs. I never told you, but I thought them real, hatchlings, peeking through the split and crack of their shells. Real beings, one boy and one girl. The girl older. Named with plainer names than had they been born overseas, continental; more pronounceable—culturally-appropriate-to-us-both names. Biblical names. I could see the boy had your green eyes, and the girl my steely grey-blue. I saw them in non-denominational state school. I saw them mannerly; but sharp. They would get your height, your health. They would get my thought, my heart; your health. They would be us 3 and 4.0 versions. They would be themselves. Independent. Inquisitive. Robust. They were as real to me as you were. So never really real. Really. They would travel, migrate. And I would have you then again for me. To walk with me. Talk with me. *As it was in the beginning...* And we always used a condom. I should have known. There would never be any more of you up inside me than you behind a sheath. I should have known. There was never, there is no animal in you—as in me—ever-ready to take flight. Soar. And I waited for that day. That day when you would come inside me. Skin in skin. Skin in skin. Skin to skin so I could really feel that exact moment when you'd come and time us to perfection. How I waited for that day. AMH dropping. Ovaries rupturing. Cervix infected. Cancerous? Pre-cancerous. HPV. Specialists saying now, *now*. Do her. Do her. DO ME NOW. And maybe, because we never got that close, you could never really have loved me, as I loved you. And oh, how I loved you. My love. I loved the gritty bits of you I hated. I loved the grit-filled bits of you that disgusted me. I even tried to love my gritted disgust of me. For you. Because you, you asked me to, my love. Oh... and how I would have done it all for you. Had you ever really loved me too. All of my days, my fertile days, were days of you.

Squiggly Arse Crack

She twists the arse of her skirt straight so the seam is in line with her crack. An off-centre skirt looks like a lopsided behind. It's bad enough having a sizeable behind, appearing unsymmetrical really just won't do. Over shoulder mirror-check of bum cheek skirt symmetry, rounder and rounder, better than fatter and fatter she supposes.

'I'll be right with you.'

Calling out to an infant as if they're a client doesn't make the most sense. She could just as easily have called out: 'Mogadishu. Tahiti. Azerbaijan.' All Squig needs to hear are undulating rhythms; sounds pitched from her mouth with her voice. If she recorded herself listing capitals and nation states could it be replayed as a lullaby?

'Ooh Baba! Two Baba! You Baba! Zoo Baba!' Whatever she hollers, Squig settles swiftly to her sounds. [Ding Dong] Conk, conk, conk—a knocking at the door. 'Rat-a-tat tat,' poking her face over Squig's crib. Clump, clump, clump as she stumbles over the labyrinth of baby junk, unpacked possessions and discarded gift wrap. Tara greets Helen:

'¡Hola!'

'¡Hola! ¿Qué tal?' Mwah, mwah. Air, cheek, air, cheek, 'Sorry, running late. No bueno.'

'S'okay, just errands. No muy importante.'

'You look fantabulous as if the baby'd had you not t'other way round.'

'In many ways ain't that the truth.' Twinkle, twinkle.

'Except in the stretch mark arena.'

Two heads nodding in Western agreement.

Clomping over the obstacle-course-cum-hallway Tara reaches a hand backwards, clasps, and guides Helen. Helen stomps, punctuating her non-guest frequent frequenter status with every elephantine footfall. The familiarity of their friendship breeds a sub-tenant-like relationship. Helen often walks around Tara's abodes as though she owns them, does things like puts Tara's kettle on and makes tea without asking. Tara doesn't find it irksome; to her it's love epitomised. Tara's homes, things, dreams, life are Helen's too. And vice versa. But Tara feels feline proprietorship of Squig, she furtively feels it. Shakes her hair in an attempt to rid maiming thoughts whenever Helen snatches her lion cub. Little Squig baby 'goos' and 'gaas'. Helen says, 'Baby poos and gas! Baby poos and gas!' Helen swipes Squig and saunters blindly through hallway maze of unpacked packing and unstacked packaging; lightly kicking this and that as if it's tit or tat.

Tara reassesses arse seam location whilst rifling through dresser drawer for keys and sunnies.

Little Squig baby 'coo-coos' for a goodbye kiss. Tara cannot dismiss Squig's charm, it decidedly disarms her, every day, in umpteen ways. Glancing around, she compares their love nest to a magpie's nest. Full of pilfered possessions from friends' annexes and quasi-stolen baby stuff. The majority of it was freecycled—to use the term lightly. Mainly it was her pecking about for what she needed and people being guilted into donating it. This nest is eclectically bedazzling. She didn't cuckoo Squig, he came here to nest with her. Although, at times, it feels like Helen may want to cuckoo little Squig baby but not like really truly… whatever.

'Do you think Squig's bum looks big in this?'

Hair flick while reclaiming rapscallion presenting nappied and swaddled derrière.

'Looks almost as if his torso and legs are one melded-together lump of body parts.'

'Yep, but does his bum look big?'

'Not at all. Completely disproportionate body shape, though. You, dear pal, have a misshapen baby who needs a trip to the baby straightening and evening out factory.'

'But his arse is a grand size. It's normal?'

'His arse resembles such, yes. But über-difficult to distinguish arse from the rest of lower half of body in swaddle suit. Perhaps ultra-thin nappy, like a panty-liner, and go-go shorts might rectify such predicament.'

'Are we now determining child's future sexual predilections as well as possible inherited body dysmorphic disorders?'

'Definite overstepping occurring, T-mate.'

'Righty-O. Sayonara.'

Tara sashays to front door and exits without looking back. It's the only way to leave Squig. If she took time and departed deliberately the only conceivable result would be stuffing Squig up her jumper and making a run for it like an athlete on LSD; where Squig could suffocate. So best to stick with sashaying out of front doors while pretending her neck is in an Elizabethan collar or pet lampshade.

o

During the lift ride to the ground floor, Tara finds cosy comfort in imagining Squig is actually up her jumper as if back in-utero. There is nothing she has ever done better than carry and bear Squig. She is so proud. He didn't fall out—miscarry. He didn't inconvenience her life—abortion. He didn't plant himself inside her in error—contraceptive failure. He wasn't the result of fourteen vodka tonics in a Mediterranean resort—inebriation. He was born with a beating heart and breathing lungs—still live. He is long and lean, has eyes that can see, ears that can hear and reflexes too. He has not simply passed the era of danger but graduated with honours—cot death. She is proud she grew him; and he her. They have grown apart together. A part of one another. Each other's intrinsically independent appendage.

Unlocking her car, she's reminded of a greeting card from the other day:

'You know your life has changed when… going to the shops by yourself is a holiday'—Motherhood.

Tara reassembles her fringe in the rear-view mirror thinking: 'Meh, it's more of a staycation than a mini-break.'

Zips to Main Street car park along parallel side street. Parks easily as she pre-noted the optimal parking and shopping times to be 10.40 a.m. to 11.55 a.m. Tuesdays, and 2.00 p.m. to 2.35 p.m. Thursdays. Before getting pregnant she'd put effort into working these things out. Practical: yes. Charts, lists and not so Stalinesque five-year plans. Supply chain management experience comes in handy all-round. She still cannot use a diaper genie, though. Googling instruction manuals is no help whatsoever.

In newsagents collecting magazine and stationery orders she passes by a babygro, it's white with black text: 'shit happens'. Hilarity. Stiffles giggles. Doesn't add it to purchases, leaves the shop, walks two storefronts down the road. 'Fuck it!' Doubles back.

Races through three other shops: haberdashery, chemist and Fairtrade coffee shop. All the while these lyrics relaying through her skull: 'Where's your mama gone? / Where's your mama gone? / Where's your mama gone? / Where's your mama gone? / …' Tara does all her grocery shopping online. Essentials and necessities get delivered of a Saturday morning in the bright and shiny SuperValu lorry, which is extra bright and extra shiny to single work-from-home mothers. 'Where's your mama gone?' refrain abruptly interjected with 'save the drama for your mama'. Now her background jingle goes: 'Where's your mama gone? / Where's your mama gone? / Save the drama for… / Where's your mama gone? / Save the drama for… / Where's your mama gone? / Save the drama for… / Where's your mama gone? / Your mama.' Rinse and repeat.

Suckling on a courtesy cappuccino Tara scootches over to nail salon. Just in time for her favourite nail artist to finish up.

'Not a pedicure just a scrape, clean, file—no paint?'

'Sure. Pay first, Tara. Chair number 4.'

Placing herself and her cappuccino in the massage chair, her feet in the water, she muses that every mother should get their feet washed once a week. It is a glorious nugget of self-indulgent time. Who has the time to spend solely cleaning their feet with a baby and chores clamouring in the background?

In the past year she has perfected the no-longer-than-five-minute-shower art. If it were to become an Olympic sport, she would bring Ireland back gold. Rump-a-thump-thump and it's all over in a few minutes. Not unlike Squig's conception, no need for commiseration, it wasn't intended to be an orgasmic experience, well, not in a sexual sense anyway. In its own way it was awesome. Feeling the implement sliding in, catching her breath, closing her eyes momentarily, making an 'O' shape with her mouth. Its very own kind of awesome. Knowing he was being planted in her to grow after all those barren years. Burrowing into her. On the screen a squiggle. Her Squig. The liberation of impregnation was better than any sexual pleasure she had experienced or could even conceive of. Freedom from waiting for 'The One' is all it's cracked up to be. Foot wash finished, her back's more discombobulated than before, from the chair's kneading; but the tension release is worth it. It's just all so worth it. Slips out the door with a 'Ta ra!' And happily in the car park lift by 11.49 a.m., back on track. Admiring her piggy toes in the 360° reflective glass it seems her arse seam skewed sideways in the mall. 'Ahhh, fuck a duck.'

Mobile phone pings:

Ruairí's shit, showered & shaved

Janey, he's grown up this past
hour ;)

He'll be out d door on 1st date
next

Bow chicka wow wow

Snapping phone shut, her staycation brusquely concluded, Tara's engine rumbles homewards to Squig.

Axis

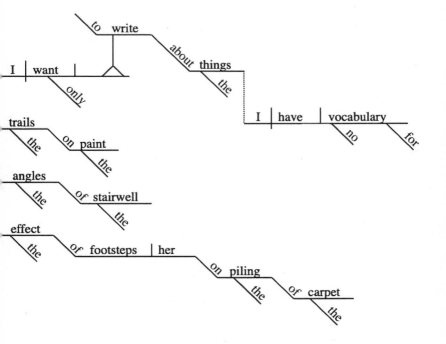

Let Ashore

On one of the now established Thursday nights, since we moved our whole tribe back home to Dublin from Manchester, Des says to me over two pints of Guinness out the back in O'Hara's *You're flighty as shite.* I say *D'ye mean nervous?* Des repeats *No flighty. You are.* I'm like *They do say I'm more responsible nowadays. There was a bulletin on 98FM after the traffic report this week — you must've missed it.* A drizzle of rain is starting and we're sitting on a sofa in the partially roofed beer garden, the one good thing the boom has brought to Ireland—posh smoking areas. Des peers over his glasses. He goes on *It's the changeable weather, it gets to you, as soon as there's a break in it, you do be off.* I look around me, feigning disorientation. I'm almost like: I have settled down. This is me settled. But I nestle into his underarm and say *How can shite be flighty?* Des insists *Do you ever get out of that head of yours?* He lights me a cigarette. I smoke. Then I'm like *No. It's with me all the time.*

Halfway through our pints I'm like *There's a class on marbling effects for ceramics, next Saturday. You free for the kids?* He squints at me, pinched face. *Would you not just hire an interior designer? You know loads of creative types.* I throw him an evil and gulp on my pint. Inside I'm screaming: I am a creative type! I am a creative type! I am a creative type! Only *It's Irish-based. I want to try my hand to the markings rain can make on solids* comes out. He goes *Ah fuck's sake, Clíodhna. You know well that's the Bank Holiday Saturday.*

Did we not book that off; together? I light up. I'm watching a couple under the heat lamp kissing, laughing. I go *I did, yeah. Just I want, a different studio, sometimes.* He tucks my hair behind my right ear. *Another time, Clí. They'll run it again.* He's watching me watching the couple. *They do always be on Saturdays.* He's pressing his thumb to my neck where the man is kissing her. *Next time.*

He moves my face with the man's movements of her face. *Recording studio's always booked out weekends. I never get a Saturday morning off.* He traces the curve of my cheek and cups my chin in his hand. *Next time, I said.* When her lips are kissed, he's turned me to him, he's pressing his thumb to my lips. *We could go down to Arklow for the few days? The kids love it there.* Des's verging on whingey. *It's fucking October. We'd be rained in.* I sullenly continue smoking. I motion to the glass collector we'll be having the same again, give them my best wink. *Ah, Clí. Would ye not.* He downs his pint. *Not, what?* I look to him, vainly. *You can be a right surly bitch of an evening.* Des squeezes my waist. I scoff *Isn't that how you like me?* He squeezes harder. *That'd be just like you, just like you to spoil all the fucking fun of it.* I lie my head against him, lace my fingers into his. *Isn't that how you like me?* He squeezes tight.

○

Standing with my forehead pressed to the window, shoulder to carriage door, I'm heading to work in the recording studio on the early morning train, when we slow down going past a stretch of water, I watch the breeze rearrange its surface, a series of ripples skating past, any patterns smoothed out before sense is made; a rising, a forming, nothing. This movement, this recognition of gravity in the water's body, my body, I think only of escape.

We chug on to where the water ebbs and flows. I can see myself in my new away life. A retreat of wattle and daub on the Malahide estuary—no, the one before it, Donabate. Somewhere marshy between those two with herons, bare feet and reeds, way enough away from the marina for the yachts and boutiques to keep out of sight. Constructed beyond the low-lying spit's curve—hocked downstream from a tidal current—sticking its tongue into the swash and backwash, right there in the centre of the waters, with no rickety tombolo, an artificial island of isolation.

We go over the river at Fairview, the strong lines the bollards cast on the water, while it's locked in, trickling through. The permanence of the concrete riverbank. The structures they build surrounding our waters, always forcefully held back, to direct the floods. We're inching towards the station. We go slower, creeping, almost no movement whatsoever, I'm certain we are stopping; I press and press and stab at the green button. *No light, love. Not stopped.* Whooshes of air explode from my lips, fogging up the window. I fight the urge to slump to the floor. As soon as we reach Connolly I dash off the train, hurry down, out to street level.

o

Instead of coming home sick from work, I check into a hotel with one of those ice bucket machines in the hallway. I feign a vice-like headache. I did have one. An idea of one. I curl up over the warp and the weft of their 400+ thread count.

In my half-sleep, I'm convincing myself home was too many hours away. There was collecting the dog from the vet, calling in on my dad to check if he'd eaten the dinners I'd dropped in for him on the weekend and seeing how many needed replacing. Getting the kids from my respective sisters-in-law. The no-longer-appetising chicken chasseur in the slow cooker. There were thirty-nine kilometres of road, eighteen miles of train line and three bodies of water. Me. And, only the pull-up nappies left. There were rush mixing deadlines with strung-out musicians, excuses; there was the off switch on my phone.

I dream of Mr O'Dwyer's island lecture from St Brendan's: 'Crannógs were ancient dwellings constructed by people in lakes and inlets. Made from locally gathered materials such as timber or brush, sand, and animal dung. They were, in essence, smaller round wooden structures that could accommodate one family or an extended family. Built offshore for defence purposes they were accessed by bridge, hidden pathway, or small boat. Evidence of crannógs dating as far back as the Mesolithic era have been found. Five thousand years of history looking at you from your geography books. Numerous in Ireland, less so in Scotland, and only one so far found in Wales.' He cleared his throat and called on me. 'Well, Missy, what do you think of that?'

'Were they cave-like? I mean, were there windows? How dark were they inside? Did everyone live in the one room? Would a person ever have one all for themselves?'

'Look at Clíodhna asking questions, you lot. She's paying attention.'

He never answered me, quite the cantankerous fecker

who liked playing mind games with pupils. Learn from me, hear my words, regurgitate them; but do not ever think for yourselves. Irish Catholic secondary school in a nutshell.

A flat-roofed turret on a crannóg seems a ridiculous request, but you want somewhere high up, exposed to the elements, to lie alone pummelled by this winter's hail as it falls.

o

Wake to the ice machine's hum. It steadies you while you apply clichéd sex-red lipstick and step into the size fourteen Clery's black satin dress, which is more like a sixteen, but it was on sale and it fit. You sit at the bar in The Gresham for five hours marinating olive-Martini-soaked teeth. Eventually, he finds you. Canadian. Faded brown eyes. Tiresome 'o' sound. Your name is anecdotal, and his impossible diphthongs break the ice. Ask him if he can say Clíodhna ten times fast with a cranberry in his mouth. He asks is there a minibar in your room.

Your sex is slow.

A luxury in this age not to be wasted. It starts in the lift with a firm crotch pressed into your buttocks, a hand on your hip bone, fingers walking down the soft folds in front, biting your earlobe, knees pressing into the backs of yours tipping you forward, then steadying you up again with his thumb. Wetness eddying below the surface, in crevices, trickling down, pooling. Stepping back, waiting. Ping.

Stalk along corridor to ice machine. Take the display bucket whether it's there for the taking or not; reach in, start filling it up. His eyes on you. Waiting. Pass the bucket into his hands, fumble for your keycard. He takes a piece of ice and starts running it up your inside leg. Feel like you might die with the want of it. Extricate keycard from envelope and hold down in slot. Ice is meandered up further and your breath catches when he slips it inside you. Push down on the handle and enter the bedroom in the dark. Take gin from the minibar. Over ice, pour two doubles. Keep going. Steeping yourself in this sex, an almost cocktail. Open the curtains wide and look out onto O'Connell Street, hear it asking *Was it for this the wild geese spread?* Wink as though all of Dublin can see you. Turn your back on them. Enjoy this. Take your knickers off. Keep his gaze. Raise your hemline. Encourage him to go down on you with the statue of Charles Stewart Parnell over your left shoulder. Hope Parnell can see. Hope he's smiling now. Adulterers in arms. Do it for your country. Pull the Canadian up by his hair and push against him until you hear him groan with the hardness. Use a condom. Take him inside you. Do it again. And again until morning. Come in waves.

○

Late the afternoon after, walking through Connolly Station, think about boarding the train to Sligo, it's decades since you've been there. You wanted to abseil forwards down a man-made wooden wall, but you could see where you were going and the vertigo got you to keep both feet on the ledge. It was a secondary school trip to Delphi Adventure Centre, or is that in Mayo? Your geography's worse since you, Des and the kids moved back last year.

I board the train home and someone I used to know from the village says *How long is it you're living back home?* I do be like *Sure you never leave. It's with you all the time.*

Let yourself into the house. Check kitchen calendar; all out at a school friend's birthday party. Feel guiltless. Switch the Russell Hobbs kettle on. Gather loose tea leaves, stems and petals. Place them in your cut-glass period teapot. Fill to brim.

Open the family laptop. Lying on the keyboard is a printout of your bank statement. Des has highlighted your illicit purchases from the thirty-four hours previous and scrawled across them, in inky indigo blue fountain pen: *Clíodhna: 33. Des: 32. My turn.*

Your body. Makes you think of escape.

Hear crack and shatter. Watch your exquisite round structure break apart into three distinct pieces. See tawny water flood the granite countertop. Pouring down onto the polished concrete kitchen floor. Leaves and brush and reeds dispersed in their own waves, drowned.

Pivot

I only want to write about the things I've no vocabulary for: the trails on the paint, the angles of the stairwell, the effect of her footsteps on the piling of the carpet.

The gaps in the leaves in the dappling on the window ledge.
The palette of greens on the external canvas.
The hook of the clasp on the collar.
The refractions of daylight on the glint of the wind chime.
The shades of the cool, the hard, the wet, the soft.
The geometry of the stretch of the branches.
The peel of the bark; slim to wide.
The hang of the downturn of the lilac on the bluebells.
The fall of the birdseed.
The reach of the head of the dandelion.
The blush on the petals of the daisies.
The spring of the hind legs.
The stippling of the mosses on the wall.
The splatters of bird shit; speckled whites, greys, browns.
The ascendant glimmer of the dew drying on the spider's silk.
The spread of the ivy.
The arc of the gate.
The trill of the wingspan in flight.
The mess of paws on the gravel.

The shift of the shells on the sole of the foot.

The curvature of sea glass.
The opalescence of minerals.
The slackness of leash in hand.
The movement of the line of the shore.
The cast to the skim of the stone on the water.
The aftertaste of her spray on my lips, briny sweet.
The geography of the backwash of the lap of the waves.

Diktat/Dictate II

/ dɪk.tæt /   / dɪk'teɪt /

Churching

It is the day of the storm's starting. The sea is in soft swell under a pale grey pendant. Obese seabirds are caw-cawing, swooping up and dipping between knotted gaps in macramé clouds. A light flurry of snow pebbles swish in front of my eyes, mirroring the seabirds' directionless flight, dusting the topsoil at my feet in spilt polystyrene. I amble down the well-trod walkway to the beach. I'm glad I thought to put on my hiking boots, if I was not with child I would have been less cautious. My belly sleeps, as is common in the late mornings. I continue to the beginnings of the cliff trail and meet with the back gate at Angie's house. She waves to me from the kitchen window. I pass the raised vegetable beds adjacent to the neighbouring beach shack, it has the village's best view of the estuary, my whole life I've hoped it would go up for sale, even though I know we could never get planning permission for a house on this site, we might work out a way to use it, to be situated, here, idyllically, closer by. Angie signs putting on the kettle. A late-February daffodil bows its yellow crown at the garden's edge. I hope it will survive the snap.

Almond and vanilla scents welcome me into the hearth. I leave my coat and boots in the back porch, cross to the rocking chair, kissing her shoulder briefly.

'It won't be long now,' she says to the kettle's hum.

'Not long, no.' Pulling the blue tartan blanket over my lap I smile at my waggling fingers and toes.

'You'll be made, the makings of you. This.'

I laugh. 'Bet you say that to all the girls,' inhaling the floury smells of this flaxen-walled room.

Angie turns to me for the first time, dips the head in acknowledgment, and scrunches up her face. 'We'll let the tea draw a while.'

'First cup!' I clap my hands together with glee.

'It's not a raffle you're calling, girl.'

My aunt shuffles forward with Bakewell hunks on dainty china saucers, and empty builder-sized mustardy mugs looped through each baby finger. The mugs have a dripping glaze on their lips. I take them and set them on the edge of the range. Angie sits opposite me on the hard-backed cushionless bachelor's chair that never shifts from its designated spot.

'I've been meaning to talk to you on your own, Loretta, sooner than now—'

'Darragh likes your cakes too much, is the problem.'

'...this last trimester.'

'I never give him even half a slice of cake on a weekday.'

'Or any day.'

'Ah now. Not half. He'd match my near nine months, if he were let,' I say, rubbing my fecund belly with both hands.

Angie wrinkles her forehead and begins the dark pours, we, neither of us, take sugar or milk which is often commented on in company: 'unusual', 'inherited', 'special'. Holding mine out, she says, 'Here's your tea.'

I grasp, then look at my mother's sister with more care and attention. 'Go on, please.' She clears her throat.

'I have though, Loretta, been meaning to talk to you on your own sooner than now; about the blessing.' Angie smiles.

'Do you mean the Christening?' I ask. 'We said we'd be organising it after the baby is born, at least a month after, hear, no rushing down the aisle,' blinking my eyes in rapid succession, affectionately. 'We won't not do it, I promise, we know it matters to you, and to Darragh's side.'

'No, *your* blessing, child.'

'Ah Ange, I'm not following you at all.'

'When you will be churched.'

'Churched?'

It's my time to frown now, but it isn't slight. It is not wrinkled. There are furrows on my face.

'Mind you don't get left like that.' Angie pours in a hot sup. 'Eat your cake, sip your tea, child.'

Like all obedient children, I do as I am told.

'If your mother was with us—may she rest in peace— she would have told you sooner, but I faffed too long waiting to get you alone, and it seems bigger, more important, it's just… It's just a blessing mothers have after the baby is born—'

'For the child?'

I receive a stern look.

'Amn't I telling you now?!' She smiles, again. 'It's just you. You go to the church on an evening after you're back home from the hospital and rested, to the lady chapel, Father Deasy will know you're coming, and he'll bring you in to give you the blessing for having had the child.'

'What is this? This. Churching?… How come I've never heard of this before?'

'It's known.'

I raise my eyes. I look at Angie. I smile, a thin smile.

'Is it?'

'It is.'

'It's a blessing amongst women. And the church. A blessing for you for having had your baby.'

'Will Darragh come?'

'No, just you.'

'And Deasy will bless me and the baby?'

'Father Deasy. For the last time no, Loretta. You. Just you; but—janey mack—bring the infant with you, if you must.' Angie downs her tea.

'How is it different from a Christening?'

'Ah Jes— Janeyjaneyjaneyjaney mack. Such an inquisitive child.'

'Obstreperous?'

'Yes. I'll go on.' Angie places her hands on my knees, my lap, and says, 'Deasy. Father Deasy, will bless you, and you alone, not Darragh, not the child, it's just for you for having given birth.'

'That's bizarre.'

'Bizarre?'

'Yeah, a secret blessing through the side-door for mammies. That's me told.'

'Finally!' Angie laughs.

'But, Ange, what's the… what do they say? During. What will Father—FATHER—Deasy say over me?'

Angie takes a folded piece of paper from her cardigan pocket, unfolds by three, and reads, '*Almighty, everlasting God, through the delivery of the blessed Virgin Mary, Thou hast turned into joy the pains of the faithful in childbirth; look mercifully upon this Thy handmaid, coming in gladness to Thy temple to offer up her thanks: and grant that after this life, by the merits and intercession of the same blessed Mary, she may merit to arrive, together with her offspring, at the joys of everlasting happiness. Through Christ our Lord.'*

I suck air. Brush crumbs onto my poppy-decorated saucer.

'Right, well, that is me told.'

Angie smiles. 'Will we make a start on the laundry?'

o

I fix to leave an hour later, having pressed and folded the freshly washed linen together, a well-timed spring clean. Seabirds are circling overhead and the sky is high and still. I turn to Angie and say, 'It'll be good to get home before the weather takes up.'

She kisses my cheek. 'A smattering of nothing.' Turns and watches the seabirds swoop and soar, crying noisily over the surf, racing each other to the shelter of the rocks.

I walk the path. I reach the gate. Ice chips at my gut. I bow my head. On the powdering of snow there is red. Splatters. Too much, too red. Blood. A deep thud like an iron bar walloping my abdomen fells me. I buckle.

'Kneel! Kneel on the ground!'

She comes close behind me.

o

A congregation has gathered around the bedside in her convalescence; her aunt, sister, mother?, niece and now and again another—she thinks perhaps the parish priest. She has been awake for some time but keeps her eyelids shut as if sleep were still upon her. She does not want to talk. Not a muscle does she stir. A steady murmur encircles her. Their Mary mumblings round and round her tour, dreamlike in their soporific ways, she listens gently in a haze. Days go by. Nights do pass. These chorused prayers an endless Mass. Mary murmurs overhead louder softer above her bed. Whose verses do they speak? She is not Mary. She feels weak. She opens her mouth but cannot greet. She wishes to quiet this constant repeat continuous loop unmerciful deceit. Lying stationary under moonlit cover glimpsing stars that outside hover. How long can she lie awake faking a weightless body ache? Slowly, slowly she opens her eyes, but she hears no baby's cries. She sees instead sad faces watch her pained pinched face like a clock. Hurriedly they resume their prayers, notably averting their sad, sad stares. Mary mumblings round her bed trying to burrow inside her head. Whose verses do they speak? She is not Mary. She feels weak. She opens her mouth but cannot greet. She wishes they'd quiet this constant repeat continuous loop unmerciful deceit.

Tears lodge in her chest beneath the cleft of her breasts. Breasts that should be suckled by her kin rest heavy on her heart. She committed no sin. In holy union her body with her husband met. An infant child they tried to beget. There is leakage now. Seepage. How? Nourishment goes as the milk flows no baby to suckle no baby to show such a hard-hitting body blow. Life force trickles around her back, a baby lost not coming back. A beautiful baby she tried to grow— no harvest no infant a desperate no-show. A wombless baby a babyless womb an unchristened baby doomed to an unmarked tomb. No white coffin no funeral could they have. The baby was taken unviewable gotten rid of. To hide the pain her child was hidden no goodbye was he bidden.

No hello. They got rid of him before she woke no screams no wails her silence choked. *Perdu perdu* a private *perdu*. *Mon Dieu! Mon Dieu!* All day long she thinks of you. A childless birth returned to earth. A God-given trial. She'll remain in denial. A kick. A stir. Her heart's all aflutter—

She must grab ahold of herself now. Somehow. Or forever after remain in this bed, being waked out as though she, in fact, is dead. It will take all her wits but she must come to grips grab at this. There is always the chance of another. And this Mary mumbling must stop. It's driving her tickity tock tock mad. She'll be glad to be awake and not the ruined bearer incanted as though waked. Out. Mary mumblings round her head nearer and farther from her bed all these novenas being said and resaid and resaid and resaid and resaid. She once was replete. Completed. Now he's deleted. It is too much. It is too much. Mary murmurs to and fro how she wishes they would go up and down and far away to another world where they would stay.

Mary mumblings on and on repetitive incessantness pattering on. Pitter-pattering on. Pitter patters along an empty street with no toddling feet. No coddling no. No. No. No. Mary mumblings ransack her brain like a steam train off its rails. Why can't she stay awake? Why can't she dictate the end is late? Loretta sees snow against the window. It is comforting. She closes her mind. Mary Mary on and on can't they sing another song? Mary bore and Mary kept her only child until he left. Mary is not in this bed. Mary does not want to be dead. Loretta opens her eyes and sees the darkness. It is comforting. She closes her mind. Mary mumblings do not stop. How she wishes they had forgot. Forgot to sit. Forgot to pray. Forgot to cosset her as she lay. Mary Mary she cannot take. Another Mary and she will break. Loretta opens her eyes and sees the rain. It is comforting. She closes her mind.

o

Mary doesn't come anymore. She hears them opening then closing the door. It won't be long now. She has to wait. To raise her arms. To meet her fate.

Angie enters short and stout. Opens dresser drawers and pokes about.

'Loretta Loretta you mustn't lay, lay lay lay in that bed all day. Get up. Get up. It's time to get up. You've left your man all alone without a pup.'

Curtains wrenched eyelids drenched. Loretta opens her eyes and sees no one. It is comforting. She closes her mind.

Angie enters begins to pout. Loretta thinks she may even shout.

'Loretta Loretta the time has come. What's been and gone cannot be undone. Wake up get up do not lay in that bed not for one more day.'

o

Loretta opens her eyes.

o

Loretta opens her eyes and sees the windowsill. It is gathering dust. This is comforting. She closes her mind.

o

Loretta opens one eye.

Her mother gasps, starts to cry and rasping says:

'You'll be all right, pet. You'll be all right, darling.'

○

Loretta asks for water. Water is given. This is quenching. She closes her mind.

'How are you feeling, dear? Awful. We know. Hush. Hush. Not a word.'

'Ah look at you there, you'll be all right, love. All right. We're all here for you.'

○

Loretta felt a hand grasp at her nether regions and pull her apart. Her body caved in on itself. A slicing a stinging and pains. Harder and softer until there was nothing left.

○

Her husband was looking at her. Not right at her. There was a dearth of looking directly at her.

'You'll be all right now. You'll be all right, pet.'

She knew. She knew. She did not want to know. She could see the ice chips on the bedside locker had become a pool. The curtains were drawn around her bed in mourning. Busy baby cries pierced her eardrums from the outer reaches of the ward. Pain navigating to her centre and tying it back together again with some thin thing radiating from within. Her temple flinched. Pinched inside. Her insides' low ends burning from thighs to stomach churning. And the ice chips had melted. She had thought them so exotic somehow.

o

Her dosage now is three per day. In her midlife dotage she remains undoting.

o

Weeping seeping innards peeping out pain coils roundabout casting hazardous streams of doubt an involuntary push a gush rushes from heart's hollow to below unmitigated sorrow running up and streaming down turns the visceral round and round senseless placement inner heart inward parts dug out hallowed *kinder* part nether untethered come apart no start just pulled apart parting part from part.

o

Turmoil recoils, lay and wane. Water glistens on windowpane. Steaming streaming raindrops flow while her body's aching caverns wallow lost and lonely dreaming only of stars.

Odd hip placement becomes discordant constellation. Tongue trip, navel lip cut in a jagged seam from hip to hip. Her of her of her and her. Begotten not made. Stayed lifeless. Maimed and remained unnamed.

Peaceful clearing debris is cheering collect in a bucket and pan what's left of the embers fan the fire no desire mustn't hope. Wrench. Feel it coming. Full moon. Strumming its tune. To some it is beauty, to her it is gloom. Doomed another month. Changing tide changeling tide changing tide changing tide changeling hide. Tide changes. To be denied. 'No, nothing yet.' Time watches her tune. No listening. No fruit of her womb. If with the changing of the tide she could no longer be tied to this. Rock-a-boom-boom. A kiss no kiss. A tithe. A pound of flesh. A scythe to her insides.

Her lithe figure has returned. He lies on top of her in evening. Shakes the headboard tries to make their belly felt heartache heartfelt bellyache stop. They rerun at it not for the fun of it in the hope of planting one in it. Nothing comes of it—

The cinders are dazzling the cinders are joy she sees the remains of her stillborn baby boy. Ashes uncover shadows remake a child a-growing and aglow. Sing. Turn over the charred bits scoop out the burnt recover the debris leave off the slumped dumped rump you could be coming up trumps.

o

'O father dear father my son he is dead. No name he was given no blessing was said. No beads on his body no cross on his head. My dear child my one child my son he is dead. No tombstone was laid just pieces were suctioned disposed and awayed. I beg you dear father here as I stand. Please bless me please see me please take my hand. My child he is drifting alone in a space. Please bless us please help us please show us grace. I'm wilful I see that. I'm trying to find some solace in the distance between the stars and my mind. I'm starting to unwind. A logic a setting a structure a prayer. For my boy to be unlost for his cries to be heard. Can you dear father see how I try to recapture the sparkle the light in my eye? Help me dear father help me to say a prayer for my lost boy to lullaby pray.'

o

'Daughter, love's lost lonely your firstborn one and only. What was once in you will always be in you.'

o

'Father father excuse her she's had some hard luck. Now she's run amok. We'll take her remake her close her up tight. We'll see she's all right.'

o

Home alone. Constant drone. Incessant chores. Days do bore.

o

He drifts in the soft space in and out of two sets of gates where hell and heavens wait.

o

'He limbos my child my son's been denied. Let us bless him. Redress him. Caress him. Redo him. Stitch and sew him back together. Let us tether. His soul is lost. That is a cost too high.'

o

Loretta opens her mouth. She speaks aloud:

i'm dearly missing you /

s

t

a

r

d

r

o

p

s

are kissing you /

lullabies exist for you /

i still consist of you / and / will persist anew / for you

IMAGE DESCRIPTIONS

Diktat/Dictate I
– Diktat/Dictate written in phonemic script.
– Sound off emoji. Speaker with backwards diagonal line scoring through.
– Limbless nude figure viewed from behind. // A pastel self-portrait of the artist at work on this text.

Winona the Wicked Wanton Woman

I

Black square or rectangular shapes. Keyhole cut outs. Trackpad sketches in cut outs.
1. Stick figure stepping, arms raised, wears crown.
2. Square window, oversized cross barred window frame, flower in plant pot on right.
3. Standing bird, scratching and looking at ground, wears crown.
4. Top: Snake shape scored with vertical line. Mid: Diagonal snake shape. Bottom: Unseen sketch, covered rub out lines.
5. Top: Two small vertical lines, downturned smile, wears crown.
6. Cross with four circular squiggles near endpoints.
7. Top: Many bird squiggles.
8. White square around black square shape. Keyhole cut out in shape of key. Three white cut outs on right-side black square. Word 'keyhole' typed four times in four cut outs.
9. No keyhole. Black square, black circle, black cone; side by side.

II

10. Stick figure. Long unruly hair. Wears dress.

11. Stick figure. Emanating secretions. Naked.

12. Row of stick figures 10 & 11 side by side six times.

13. Row of stick figures 10 & 11 side by side six times.

III

14. Curved line and spermatozoon.

15. Naked body silhouette. Dots above and around breast.

16. Naked body silhouette (larger size). Dots above and around breast. Curved line and spermatozoon superimposed near pubic mound.

17. *Black square or rectangular shapes. Keyhole cut outs. Trackpad sketches in cut outs. Five keyholes in jagged row, not quite side by side.*

    1) Bottom: Four scratches.

    2) Bottom: Seven scratches.

    3) Mid: Up and down scratches on left. Cross-hatch scratches on right. Break in centre.

    4) Mid: Multitude unbroken scratches, form black scribble.

    5) Top (right): Multitude unbroken scratches, form black scribble reaching to centre.

18. Finger tracing continuous scroll on trackpad, reads: 'SleepWellLittleOnes'.

ABCB AABCCB// Untitled Child's Song

– Landscape layout, transposition of London Bridge and own text superimposed on continuous rounds of Frère Jacques.

AXIS

– Sentence diagram of text: 'I only want to write about the things I've no vocabulary for: the trails on the paint, the angles of the stairwell, the effect of her footsteps on the piling of the carpet'.

Diktat/Dictate II

– Diktat/Dictate written in phonemic script.
– Enlarged performing arts emoji. Black on white. One mask frowns. The other smiles. // Illustration of artist's sentiments on the entire collection, all stories could be reduced to a drama emoji devoid of written text.

TEXTS REFERENCED

Penitential Acts
Transposition of the *Penitential Act*; the *Hail Mary*, prayer, from the Roman Missal, Catholic Church; and own text.

Hills like Hemingway's
Transposition of 'Hills Like White Elephants' by Ernest Hemingway, 'To A Child Dancing In The Wind' by W.B. Yeats, and own text.

Winona the Wicked Wanton Woman
Verses quoted from *The Ballad of the White Horse* by G.K. Chesterton, Book I, 'The Vision of the King'.

ABCB AABCCB// Untitled Child's Song
Transposition of Frère Jacques, London Bridge, and own text.

How, I?
Quote from *Glory Be to the Father/Gloria Patri*, doxology, from the Roman Missal, Catholic Church.

Let Ashore
Quote from 'September 1913', W.B. Yeats.

Churching
Text quoted from the *Churching of Women*, rite, benedictional, Catholic Church.

PUBLICATION NOTES

Mammy Mary Says
–*The Los Angeles Review*, February 24, 2022

Hot Rocks
– Hennessy New Irish Writing, *The Irish Times*, July 30, 2016
– Inkrocí/Irish Writer's Centre, *Magazine of Literatures*, N. 23, March/April, 2017 (in English with Italian translation)

Hills like Hemingway's
– *Irish Times Books*, May 25, 2018

Pinna
– *The Cormorant Broadsheet*, Issue 6, ed Niamh Mac Cabe, 2021

The First Person Possessive Or Proper Nouns Are Lost To The Yesterdays We All Dreamt Of Anyway
– *gorse*, Issue 11, ed. Susan Tomaselli, forthcoming

Phonology
– *Lighthouse Literary Journal*, Issue 13, 2016

Joni Mitchell Nudes
– *Lighthouse Literary Journal*, Issue 17, 2018

Molly & Jack at the Seaside
– *Still Worlds Turning*, No Alibis Press, ed. Emma Warnock, 2019

Squiggly Arse Crack
– *The Trouble with Flying and Other Stories*, Margaret River Press, 2014

ACKNOWLEDGEMENTS

I'd first like to thank my family. Most of all my mother, Patricia, who has always loved reading, and taught me to read and write. My dad, Gerry. My sister, Deborah. My brother, Keith. My late brother, Justin. And Jayne Colman for being my always-sister. I have a large extended family who I love; so thank you, and you, and you, and you too ... To my late grandmother, Essie, thank you for telling me you were proud of my book reading, learning and teaching—it is some great thing to know my Nanny felt pride in me.

My thanks to my friends and readers and my reader-friends.

Maria Coscoran, my best childhood friend. Thank you for the love, thank you for the giggles.

Lindsay Ruigrok, my first ever reader and pear, and Britta Baer, my second ever reader and lobster. Lindsay, *Pinna*, I could not have done this or accomplished anything if I hadn't had your wholehearted love in my life, how lucky we have been to be lifelong pears and apples together. Brit, from the first moment I met you, I loved you; you are the other half of me. *Alma gemela* x

Eoghan Bonass, GRMMA for urgent image-aid. My dear dear homeboy, you are one in a trillion. Lorraine Giblin, a genuine *Starbar*. Damien Murphy, for constant friendship, help with metre for rhyme, pints, gin and wine. Fiorella Ormeño-Incio, my Geppetto. Brian Edwards. Stephanie Ní Thiarnaigh, for reading, Gaeilge, and being the kindest stranger I have ever met.

Gizem Açelya Aykan and Radka Panayotova, my Canterbury crew. Ruth Wyer, my bessie mate, for reading every redraft as incisively as the first; for generosity and sanctuary. Helen Ferguson, for kintsukuroi and linguistics. Marianne Caren, for caring and needles. Louise Omer, *do chroí agus anam*.

June Caldwell, for your exceptional mind, daily doses of reality, empathetic clairvoyant heart, aubergines and rainbows. And, Özgecan Kesici, for your brilliance that shines so brightly from you, for art, for the chats and always for cake.

Thanks to my Fly brethren without whom this book would have drowned in a sea of my own tears. To Brooks Group, for crits on *The Perfect Flick*.

For their support and encouragement my heartfelt thanks to Lia Mills, Sinéad Gleeson, Sarah O'Neill, Denis Kehoe, Joanna Walsh and Susan Tomaselli. Anna De Vaul. Maggie O'Farrell. For timely encouraging words of wisdom my thanks to Bryony Lavery and Mary Dorcey. To Nuala Ní Chonchúir for naming Barry's character, and for solidarity.

Love and thanks to Rush Dramatic Society and The Millbank Theatre where I first fell for art. Dr PJ Mathews for answering a random question about oranges in 1990s Irish Literature. Sarah Helen Kendall. The Nomadic Players. Aberystwyth University, Dr Tiffany Atkinson and Dr Mathew Francis.

Kensington & Norwood Writers' Group for their support with the infancy of this book – way back when in the land of Oz. Margaret River Press, for my first published story; to Caroline and John Wood for their hospitality. Dr Anna Solding for telling a jaded unpublished me: 'I love your writing'. Everyone at Writers South Australia and the entire team in Varuna.

All from the Irish Writers' Centre. Sue Booth-Forbes at

Anam Cara. Paul Maddern at the Rivermill. The terrific team at Annaghmakerrig.

Thank you to Emma Warnock for liberating Molly from my laptop. The poor woman had been living there sexually frustrated since 2004, no word of a lie; 2004. David Torrans and everyone at No Alibis Bookstore and Press; it is my absolute pleasure to know and work with you.

Fingal Feminist Network.

The Arts Council of Ireland and Fingal County Council Arts Office for the bursaries that kept a roof over my head.

Sharon Blackie for so very, very much. Simon Ashfield-Smith and Anne Marie Toole.

To Sallyanne Sweeney, my agent, who is most kind and therefore my pleasure to work with.

My thanks to Sanya Semakula and Gary Budden for saying yes. Sanya, Dan Coxon and Trudi Suzanne Shaw for compassionate editing. Vince Haig for piecing it all together. Sukruti Anah Staneley for her exquisite cover. And, the lads at Influx Press for all they do for art.

Thank you to bookshops and libraries and trains and technology. To beaches for walking my dog, Caoimhe, on.

Thank you daydreamers and artists. To writers for writing; I am always writing in conversation. So thank you, thank you for your work. Thank you for the conversation.

ABOUT THE AUTHOR

Lauren Foley (she/her) is Irish/Australian and bisexual. Her stories are published internationally. She has Systemic Lupus Erythematosus (SLE) and is disabled; the majority of her writing is dictated. In 2016, her story 'K-K-K' won the inaugural Neilma Sidney Short Story Prize with *Overland* Literary Journal and was shortlisted for the Irish Book Awards Short Story of the Year. She was shortlisted for the Hennessy New Irish Writer of the Year in 2017, and nominated for The Pushcart Prize. Lauren was awarded a prestigious Next Generation Artist's Award in Literature from the Arts Council of Ireland in 2018, and subsequent Artist's bursaries. She is the recipient of two Varuna Fellowships, two Tyrone Guthrie Residencies and a Cill Rialaig Residency. Her work *'I Don't'* is published in, *The Art of the Glimpse*, 100 Irish Short Stories, ed. Sinéad Gleeson. She won *The Los Angeles Review* 2021 Literary Award in Creative Non-Fiction with *Mammy Mary Says*.

INFLUX
PRESS

Influx Press is an independent publisher based in London, committed to publishing innovative and challenging literature from across the UK and beyond.

Lifetime supporters: Bob West and Barbara Richards

www.influxpress.com
@Influxpress